Daymares

KENYA MOSS-DYME

Copyright © 2014 by Kenya Moss-Dyme

Second Edition

Cover design/Graphics: Kenya Moss-Dyme

This novel is a work of fiction. Any resemblances to actual events, real people, living or dead, organization, establishments, locales are products of the author's imagination. Other names, characters, places, and incidents are used fictitiously.

All rights reserved. No part of this book may be used or reproduced in any form or by any means, electronic or mechanical, including photocopying, recording or by information storage and retrieval system without the written permission from the publisher and writer.

Because of the dynamic nature of the Internet, any Web addresses or links contained in this book may have changed since publication and may no longer be valid.

The views expressed in this work are solely those of the author and do not necessarily reflect the views of the publisher and the publisher hereby disclaims any responsibility for them.

Contents

Dedications	1
Junebug/The Flat Earth	3
A Colder Kind of Hell	33
1st of the Month	71
Playground	131
Ride	149
Her Things	171
Baby Mine	193
Acknowledgments	284
About Kenya	285
Join My Mailing List	286
More by Kenya	287

Get SICK with me!	288
Reviews matter.	289
Find Me. Follow Me.	290

Dedications

My children – Nate, Brittany and Joseph: I couldn't love anyone or anything as much as I love you guys. And I wouldn't change a thing.

Marla Jackson: You were the first to read and praise Patchwork, lighting the flame. Nearly 30 years later, you still had the original, typewritten copy and here I can't even find the earrings I wore yesterday. They just don't make teachers like you anymore. I hope I've made you proud.

ExModSquad – Felicia, Sandra, Jeannie and Sylvia: Who said online friendships aren't real? Sixteen years and counting...

My sister – My friend. I love you for your unwavering support in everything I do.

Foreword

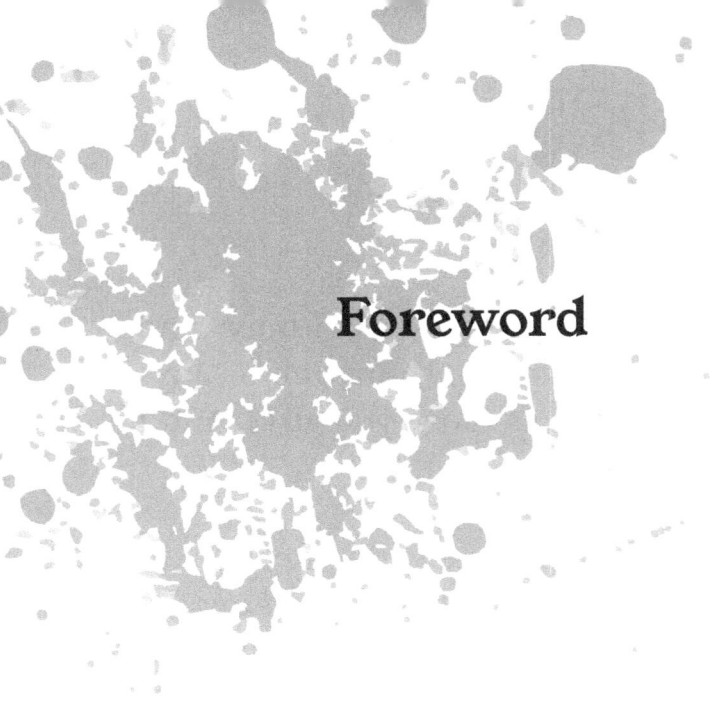

Stepmothers often get a bad rap in fiction. I've had a few stepmothers that were pretty awful but I also had one that was a blessing. Then I became a stepmother to two little girls – one loved me with all of her heart; the other wanted me to just disappear into thin air and would do anything to make it happen. So I've been on both ends of the step-parenting issue. In horror stories, it's always the evil stepmother that causes the conflict, but sometimes the stepchild has their own agenda.

Junebug/The Flat Earth

TENDING THE GARDEN WAS the only thing that ever calmed her nerves. It took her away from the madness indoors and a quiet peace draped over her head and shoulders like her favorite blanket. As soon as her knees touched the soft soil, her blood pressure decreased and her breath slowed. Waving her fingers through the spread of green leaves had a calming effect that no little white pill could provide.

The fresh smell of foliage filled her nostrils and she inhaled deeply, feeling the energy return and course through her body. Her arms and legs were tingling now; she used her gloved hands to smooth over the open patch of soil where no flowers yet appeared.

The seeds buried beneath would begin peeking out in a few days with just a little love and care, bolstered by sunshine. The Morning Glories would be a nice addition to the little garden, it needed more color; she had stuck to mostly greenery since it was in the back of the house and no one would see it behind the privacy fence. But she had suddenly been inspired to add some color, hence the Morning Glory seeds.

She rose from the ground carefully, wincing at the pain in her hip, and retrieved the water sprayer to moisten the bare patch. Relief flooded through her veins like the water rushing from the hose. Watching the dirt turn black with needed moisture, she smiled. Her garden hadn't truly pleased her in some time and she'd become bored with it, but this - this gave her joy again.

The sound of a car door slamming jolted her from her thoughts. The king was home! She reached down and slapped the dirt from her knees before peeling off her gardening gloves and placing them on the little stool. One final step before she could return to the house; she ducked into the little shed and looked around the shelves, moving the cans of engine oil and plant fertilizer, until her hand closed around the wooden end of the sign.

The pole sunk smoothly into the wet dirt until it struck solid and could go no further.

"Carlita!" The king bellowed through the house and she scrambled to clean up her tools before going to greet her husband. She could hear him moving about the kitchen, lifting the lids on the pots to see what she had assembled for dinner.

"Did you wash your hands?" She yelled at him from the laundry room where she peeled off her dirty clothing and slipped into a t-shirt and gym shorts. She'd removed her sweaty bra and panties and rummaged through the clean basket for fresh replacements, but there was nothing but the King's laundry and Junebug's play clothes.

She sighed and limped slightly on her way into the kitchen in her bare feet with her breasts jiggling underneath the thin t-shirt.

He turned to look at her when she entered and his eyes fell immediately to her chest.

"Dessert?" He asked with a grin, stretching out his hand to touch her.

She slapped him away.

"Dessert is after dinner, right?"

"Doesn't have to be - we make our own rules," He reached out quickly and pinched her nipple before she could duck away from him.

"Where's Junebug? We can sneak upstairs real quick before he notices - I won't take long!" He looked behind him to see if his son was sneaking up on him as he usually did when he returned from work. Carlita used his distraction as a chance to escape the reach of his long arms, although the idea of a quickie was appealing and she felt her thighs tremble slightly at his touch. The sharp pinch reminded her that his tenderness was conditional upon her accepting his reality and foregoing her own.

She went to the stove and began stirring the pot of thick tomato sauce for the pasta. Bubbles rose to the surface and she caught a glimpse of a curly brown hair floating on the top before it dipped beneath the surface again. She used the spoon to tap at the bubbles to see if it would pop up again so she could lift it out, but it never reappeared.

"Babe, hand me that foil-covered bowl from the fridge, please," Carlita said over her shoulder.

King opened the fridge and removed the large bowl, then lifted a corner of the foil to take a sniff.

"Chicken?" He asked, poking at it with his finger.

"Hey! Again - did you wash your hands?" Carlita took the bowl and dumped the contents across the pan of freshly blanched pasta noodles, then swished the yellow chunks of meat around with a spatula before spreading a layer of shredded cheese over the top.

"Junebug! Junebug, I'm home!" King bellowed through the house.

"Stop yelling! He's probably inside Timmy's house, he'll be here eventually."

"But he always comes home when I get off from work - that's our time."

Carlita smirched. "Yeah, I know, *your* time. How could I forget?"

"Aw, don't be jealous - I offered you a ride on the magic stick before he got here; I was going to put on a cartoon to keep him busy but you turned me down," King slapped her butt and pulled out his cell phone.

"What's Timmy's mom's number? I'll call and tell him to get here."

Carlita covered his hands with her own to stop him from dialing, then gently removed the phone from his fingers and dropped it into her pocket.

"Baby, let him play! He's getting older; you gotta stop treating him like a baby. He doesn't need to come home and be tossed in the air like a toddler. They're probably playing Xbox or something."

King frowned and rubbed his bearded chin, thinking. He looked forward to bonding with the boy every evening and he was more than a little disappointed to see that Junebug may be focusing his interest elsewhere.

They had been through a lot, those two. They were both still grieving the loss of Junebug's mother to a drunken driver, less than two years earlier when Junebug was merely three years old. Carlita had been one of the unit nurses in the hospital where his first wife finally succumbed to her devastating injuries. She breezed into their lives and helped settle the storm during the frenzy of the lawsuits, trial and sentencing of the driver. She brought a certain peace to their home and King was able to return to his job as a police officer, assured that Junebug was in good hands.

Carlita had no children of her own. She was a few years older than King and fell in love with him the moment she looked into his eyes. He was frantic over the possibility of losing his wife and his hands shook so much that he couldn't hold on to the papers she'd handed to him. She covered his shaking hands with hers and assured him that he didn't need to worry about paperwork at that moment.

Tears flowed down his cheeks as he thanked her and shuffled back into his wife's bed in the intensive care room. Carlita stayed on all night to make sure he had what he needed and that the other nurses gave him the highest level of attention. When his wife failed to recover from her internal injuries, she was there to help him with the details and preparations, easily sliding into the role of friend and eventually lover.

But Junebug wasn't giving in so easily. He was a problem from day one. With his big brown eyes and protruding teeth that were just a little too big for his mouth, he was determined to be sullen and difficult. Perhaps in allegiance with his dead mother, he didn't want to love or even *like* another woman in her place. She'd tried so hard, she wanted to be a good mother but he refused to accept her offerings.

So they danced daily. She'd rise early to make his favorite chocolate and caramel pancakes; have them sitting on a warm plate for his breakfast, and he'd sit at the table and cross his arms and stare, refusing to eat.

Birthdays came and went and a corner of the basement began to pile up with unopened presents - things that Carlita had purchased and wrapped lovingly for the boy. He didn't want them. He refused to eat the cake, declined the gifts, and sat staring off into space with his eyes tight, chewing on his lower lip, while the party went on around him.

King shrugged it off; he never wanted to get involved, thinking that Junebug just needed a little understanding; the adjustment was rough for him. *Don't push him,* King advised. *Give him more time.* Two years later, Carlita was still spending each day desperately plotting and strategizing on how to win Junebug's love.

"Mmmmm, that smells good already! When can we eat?" King opened the oven door and peeked inside.

"Junebug loves chicken - he's gonna love this - let me call him-"

"Don't you dare!" Carlita turned on him with her eyes ablaze. "I told you to leave him alone! You wanted him to have a friend, he finally has a friend, now leave him alone and let him play!"

King recoiled in surprise. "Gee, sorry. Didn't mean to piss you off!"

He stepped away from the stove and slumped into a dining chair.

Carlita threw her arms around his shoulders and covered his huge neck with kisses.

"I just really want to make this evening special, I want Junebug to be in a good mood for a change and I want us to enjoy dinner together – like a family!"

King twisted in his seat so he could look into his wife's eyes. A tear slid down her cheek as he cupped her chin in his hand.

"Honey, I know you've been trying so hard, its okay," He said soothingly as he stroked her face. "I'll step back from this one and let you run the show. Maybe that's part of the problem, I always try to jump in and redirect things, to keep you from getting hurt. Maybe I need to just let you and Junebug work it out on your own."

Carlita nodded. "I think that would help a lot. As long as he knows that you are going to defend him, he doesn't have to try to be nice to me."

"Okay, I'll stay out of it, starting today. Promise."

"Thank you, babe. You'll see, he'll be inviting me to Mother and son dances soon!"

"Ha! That I'd like to see!"

"Just wait, he's got to give in at some point, it takes far more energy to hate me than it does to love me." Carlita playfully slapped his massive arm and returned to her cooking.

"He doesn't hate you, he just misses YoYo, it's been hard for him."

"And it's been hard for me as well," insisted Carlita with a frown. "But I'm doing my best. I've been patient but I'm human, I have feelings too."

"He's a child, Carlita, he's not emotionally mature enough to understand what he's doing. He sees you as competition for me – and I'm all he's got left," said King.

"Don't make excuses for him, Honey. It's not okay to be rude to me, even if he doesn't want to love me or like me – YoYo should have taught him to respect his elders."

King scowled at the criticism of his dead wife. "Watch yourself now. I told you before, don't go there and we'll be fine."

He took a water bottle from the fridge and left the kitchen angrily. She had crossed that line unintentionally but it was too late to unspeak those bitter words. She didn't actually bear any ill will against Junebug's mother, how could she? She never knew her. She had only seen her when she was brought into the hospital the night of the accident, the night she was assigned to her care and delivered her final dose of morphine before she slipped away, and then at her funeral. But she was resentful of the bond that Yoyo seemed to have with Junebug even after death.

At times it felt as if she were controlling Junebug from the grave, coaching him on how to respond to every conversation with his new stepmom, how to make her feel every bit as useless and intrusive as possible. No matter what she tried to coax some kind of acknowledgment, hug or even a smile, he blocked her at every turn.

Carlita soon accepted that Junebug may never see her as anything more than an invasion into his life, and she was learning to be fine with that. It was a tradeoff for the fortune she gained by marrying King.

But when Junebug tried to kill her, she knew she was dealing with more than just a sad little boy.

King insists that it was just an accident, but Carlita knew better. Accidents happen, certainly, but the car slipping into reverse while Carlita walked behind it – that was no accident. She was headed to the mailbox at the end of the drive and as she turned slightly to wave at the neighbor, she caught a brief flash of movement in the rear window. It happened too fast to register in her brain the connection between Junebug being buckled in the backseat and the car suddenly lurching backward down the driveway toward her, bumping her hip as she dove into the grass. It narrowly missed crushing her under its wheels.

Carlita's body healed over time, leaving her with the permanent limp, but her heart didn't forget so quickly. At King's insistence, she put aside her feelings and instead focused on not making Junebug feel bad about the accident. So she never said a word about seeing Junebug scoot across the backseat of the car just as it began to roll toward her.

She never mentioned it because she knew that King wouldn't believe her. But when she nearly overdosed on her pain medication, it all came bubbling up from her throat and spilling across her lips before she could stop it.

"I didn't take too many pills, King, I'm a nurse, for God's sake, I know how to fucking medicate myself!"

King stood next to her hospital bed looking down at her pitifully.

"We all make mistakes, Hon," He said.

"God-dammit, King! Do you really think I accidentally took too many pain killers? Do you think I'm that stupid?"

King rubbed his forehead then scratched furiously at his beard.

"I didn't say you were stupid, I'm just saying, you've been in a lot of pain – maybe you were a little confused, pain can make you feel all out of sorts –"

"Maybe Junebug put something in the glass he brought me to take the fucking pills!" Carlita screamed at him.

"What is that supposed to mean?"

"What don't you get? He brought me a glass of milk to take my pills and now look where I wake up – coincidence?"

King's eyes widened. "You...are really losing it. Junebug said you were acting strange earlier – and now this."

"Look just get the fuck out and let me rest. I'm not dead yet so you and Junebug can go plot something else for me," Carlita turned her back to him and pulled the thin hospital sheets up around her neck, effectively dismissing him and ending the conversation. She listened for the sound of his shoes as he exited the room; then she started to silently cry. The sweet smell of the lilacs in her garden wafted through the open window and gave her comfort.

King watched her closely when she came home the next day, taking a few weeks off work so he could care for her. He was there at every turn, bringing her meals, massages on demand, brushing her hair while she lay across his lap. It was blissful and serene, almost like the early days of their marriage when he would barely let her feet touch the floor.

When King returned to the business of running his company, Junebug stepped up his efforts to eliminate her.

The following weeks brought a tumble down the stairs, a narrow escape from a sudden gas leak behind the dryer, and a close shave with the electric carving knife.

After so many *accidents*, Carlita asked King for a dog.

"What are you going to do with a dog, my love?" King asked, looking at her as if she had asked for a wild leopard.

"Just for companionship, I get lonely here during the day. Besides, dogs are great for smelling gas and detecting danger, the hospital works with this group that gives dogs to patients who need assistance."

"Well, you do need assistance, that's for sure," said King. "You've been a walking zombie since the accident with the car!"

Carlita winced at his words.

"Yeah, *the accident*," she said.

"Don't start," King rolled his eyes and threw back the bed covers to leave.

"Junebug, come here, baby boy!" King's deep bass cut through the quiet morning.

Carlita struggled to pull herself up higher on her pillow. "What are you calling him for?"

"To tell him the news, that you guys are getting a dog!" King bounced on the bed like a child; like a six and a half foot bearded child.

Junebug suddenly appeared in the doorway with his usual scowl. He never made noise as he moved through the house; it was as if he *floated* when he walked, his feet didn't seem to touch the floor, because Carlita never heard him approach.

He stood there with his eyes fixed on Carlita; she pulled the blanket up to her neck and stared at the blank television screen.

"Hey, Son! Good news! You're getting a dog!" King announced with glee. "What kind of dog do you want?"

Junebug continued to stare, soundlessly.

"You don't have to tell me now, tell me when I get home from work and we can go pick it out this weekend," King walked over to hug his son and the boy circled his arms around King's waist with affection while peering around his body to stare coldly at Carlita. She looked away when she saw him smile.

A few days later, King came roaring into the house cradling a miniature schnauzer against his massive chest.

"What the hell is this?" Carlita asked, lightly stroking the tiny head of the pup.

"You asked for a dog – I got you a dog – what's the problem now?"

"I wanted a DOG, King – not a toy! This is a TOY, I don't need something to play with!" Carlita yelled through tears.

"What else do you need a dog for? I thought you wanted a companion? That's what you said!" King had already started moving through the house, looking for Junebug.

"I wanted a big dog, not a little tiny rat, for heaven's sake, King, why didn't you ask me what I wanted? Why would you go and get it yourself without even asking me?"

She collapsed into the nearest chair and bent over into her own lap and cried; she waited to feel his big hands on her back, soothing and comforting her, but she could only hear him in the next room talking excitedly with Junebug about what they would name *their* new pet. That tiny thing couldn't protect her at all! She wanted something big and terrifying, something that would guard her at night when King wasn't home, so she could finally sleep peacefully. This little rat dog was not at all what she had in mind!

Carlita decided then that she'd had enough. If King would not take her side, she would have to stand up for herself. She wiped her tears with the corner of her shirt and joined them in the next room.

"That's MY dog, I asked for it, so it's mine," she said as she entered. "I'm going to name it Poppy. Thank you." Carlita walked between them and picked up the tiny animal, leaving the room with her husband and stepson staring at her back.

She didn't expect King to stop her. He didn't even try. She could hear them whispering behind her back as she walked away.

The next day, she called a friend to give her a ride to the animal shelter, where she traded Poppy for Dingo – a big, beast of a monster with sharp teeth and even sharper claws. He stood as tall as Junebug with a ferocious bark – and he fell in love with the boy as soon as Carlita brought him inside.

She bitterly watched them bond with each other on the front lawn, as much as Junebug knew how to bond with something living; he stood next to Dingo rubbing its head while Dingo eagerly reached up and licked his arm.

Carlita left them alone and went inside to change into her gardening clothes. She needed to feel the earth between her fingers to keep from breaking down in frustration. She could hear Dingo barking happily and Junebug was silent, as usual, but she imagined he was enjoying himself by commandeering *her* dog; he probably had that same sick smile plastered on his face. It was surprising that Dingo liked him – dogs are supposed to be able to detect evil.

After pruning the dead leaves from the Hostas and spraying plant food across the flower bed, she stood back to admire her work. She had plans for the empty patch in the middle and felt anxious to get started seeding; it always excited her to plant because it gave her a chance to create and nurture, and to have something rely on her for its existence. She missed that since having to leave her position at the hospital; she missed having people need her, but with all of the accidents, her body wasn't able to handle the long shifts and continuous walking.

The barking quieted.

Carlita walked around to the front of the house to take a peek at Junebug and Dingo but they had moved from the front lawn and were nowhere in sight.

She went inside through the front door and walked into the living room, then froze.

Junebug sat in the overstuffed chair with the barrel of the pistol pointed directly toward Carlita; the gun was heavy and he balanced the weight of the handle with both of his little hands.

"What-what are you doing, Junebug? Please, put that down, please!" Carlita spoke softly, slowly and raised her hands out in front of her body, palms displayed in a sign of surrender. She was afraid to scare the boy and he might accidentally pull the trigger....*accidentally.*

"Where did you get that gun?" Carlita whispered. "That's nothing to play with, Junebug. Put it down on the table next to you slowly – I don't want you to get hurt. I don't want to get hurt! You're really scaring me right now."

Junebug didn't move. He held the gun steady – terrifyingly steady for a 6 year old who supposedly had never held a gun. *Or had he been practicing for this moment?*

Dingo lay on the floor next to the chair with his head resting on his paws; he whimpered softly as if he could detect the danger in the air. Carlita prayed that he wouldn't react and jump.

"Please, Junebug, put it down, *baby*." The word didn't even feel right coming out of her mouth. She hadn't called him baby since they first met, back when she believed he was just a sweet sad little boy. Now, she knew better, and if she still wasn't sure – looking down the barrel of her husband's gun made it clear.

Junebug sneered at her over the top of the big gun. His little fingers twitched as if he was having a hard time not *holding* the gun but keeping himself from pressing on the trigger. His eyes twinkled and the tip of his tongue snaked out to moisten his lips.

At that moment, Carlita knew she was about to die. Every nerve in her body relaxed when she hear loud music blasting into the driveway as King arrived home from work. She tried to force a smile at Junebug to keep him from panicking and *jerking*.

"Your dad's home, Junebug," she whispered. "Let me help you put that away so he doesn't have to know about this, okay?"

King slammed the car door. In minutes, he would be coming through the front door. Carlita didn't want to move but she didn't want King to burst into the house in his usual loud and boisterous manner. At the same time, perhaps him catching Junebug like this would finally show him the truth about his son; finally proving that Carlita wasn't hysterical or just having trouble adjusting to being a mom. He would see the *real* Junebug, the demonic child that held her hostage in her own home.

Junebug slowly lowered the gun to his side and pushed it down into the side of the cushion. He hopped out of the chair and his little legs carried him quickly and silently out of the room, leaving Carlita standing there feeling an overwhelming sense of both shock and relief.

King entered the house and came up behind her and slapped her playfully on her ass.

"What are you standing there for?" He asked as he passed her and headed down the hallway.

She waited for the sound of him closing the bathroom door before rushing to the chair. The handle of the gun felt warm in her hands and she realized with a shiver that she hadn't just walked in and surprised Junebug; he had been sitting there for a long while, holding the gun, *waiting* on her to come through the door.

"What is *wrong* with that stupid dog?" King rose and stumped through the kitchen to the back door. "Shut it up, Dingo!" He roared through the screen.

The dog ignored him and continued barking and snarling at whatever was upsetting him.

"Dammit!" King swung open the door and stormed out into the yard. Carlita cringed at the thought of what he might do to the dog once he got his hands around his neck; her breathing slowed as she listened to him screaming in the back of the house. Dingo welped in pain; King had caught him and it wasn't to rub his head and give him a treat.

"I said, shut it up!"

Dingo welped again.

The door swung open and hit the wall as King returned. Dingo began barking again.

"What's wrong with him?"

"I don't know! He kept digging in your garden and I kicked his ass! I told you we shoulda got rid of him a long time ago!"

The room was spinning; Carlita tried to grab the counter to balance herself but she put her weight on the open drawer, sending the hundreds of pieces of silver crashing to the floor around her feet.

"What the hell?!" King jumped. "Need some help there?" He asked, before settling back into his seat.

King raised his hand to take another bite of his food and froze with his fork suspended in mid-air.

Junebug stood on the threshold leading to the backyard; his head was down, looking at the floor. Dingo sniffed around at his feet, whimpering now, pawing at the mud on Junebug's shoes.

"Junebug –" King's voice faltered as his eyes took in the image of his son.

His clothing was soaked, dark and sticky as clumps of wet soil fell from his body to the floor around his feet. He trembled ever so slightly and more dirt fell from his curly hair, tumbling down the front of his shirt and landing on the tops of his sneakers.

When he raised his head and fixed his eyes in Carlita's direction, she screamed. Eyes white in a pale and bloodless face; unfocused, staring…accusing. His lips parted and formed a snarl, as unintelligible words tumbled over his tongue and stung Carlita's face.

He moved forward slowly with a lopsided shuffle, the left side of his body hung awkwardly as he seemed to drag himself across the floor toward Carlita. When he reached her, he threw himself forward against her legs and she reached out to catch him.

Junebug reached up for her with a cold dirty arm and beckoned her to bend closer; she trembled as she leaned toward him.

"My turn," Junebug whispered in her ear before her legs gave out and she fell to the floor, her body straddling the scattered pile of silverware.

Foreword

Like many people, I often watch court shows and live trial proceedings and wonder just how criminal defense attorneys can stand in front of the courtroom and proclaim their clients to be innocent. Especially when the client was caught on security camera committing the crime and posing for a selfie with the dead body, while wearing their work uniform and name badge. Yet, their lawyer will stand in front of the jury with a straight face and say, "My client was framed!" That has always completely fascinated me! I wonder if their passion for justice might change if their viewpoint was more of an empirical nature?

A Colder Kind of Hell

Time to make the donuts, time to make the donuts!

Melody chanted softly to herself as she drove to the little donut shop near her house. It wasn't her favorite job, and it certainly wasn't part of any career plan, but it paid the bills and helped her make small but steady moves toward her real dream of becoming a celebrity makeup artist.

As a small child, she loved playing in her mother's makeup and using it to paint the faces of her dolls. She occasionally painted her own, but her mother would scold her and make her wash it off, saying that it made her look "fast". She didn't know what fast meant at that young age, but she loved the way she look after she smeared her face with the brightly colored sticks and creams from her mother's dresser.

Eventually, she learned some things about the makeup, like how important it was to replace the caps after every use - her mother was angry more than a few times after finding her expensive products dried out or spilling across the dresser.

Melody also learned which colors looked best together, which ones were easiest to apply and remove, and which ones could be mixed together to create even prettier colors. She learned how to draw lines with precision and smooth the creamy butters until you couldn't tell it was makeup, your face just looked flawless.

By the time she was 17, her mother became her biggest fan and first client. She paid her to do her makeup for an important business meeting and she came home smiling from ear to ear. She had tears in her eyes when she came home and hugged Melody tightly.

"Thank you for making me feel like the most confident and beautiful woman in the building!" Her mother said in her ear as she held her.

"You're going to go far, Melody," she told her, holding her face in her hands. "Do you hear me? Whatever you need, Mama is going to get it for you. I'm going to make sure you accomplish your dream!"

It was then that Melody knew she had to step out into the real world with her talent, but she would need to take some classes to get certified so she could work in a salon and participate in hair and fashion shows. From there, she could be noticed by a celebrity who would hire her to be their personal makeup artist and take her on all of their appearances.

But first, she had to make enough money to purchase her professional tools and pay for makeup artist classes.

So on this day, like the previous 97 days, she was driving to the donut shop. It was boring and repetitive work, standing at the counter all day, putting donuts into boxes and ringing up sales, but she was *this* close to paying for a titanium flat iron, so she put a smile on her face and went to work every day without complaint.

Pulling into the parking lot, she took note of her coworker's cars; that's how she judged the quality of each day at work by the others working her shift. She recognized the car belonging to Cornelia, an older woman who was loved by all of the staff; Chris, the shift manager who was not so loved by the staff; Jodi, a 16 year old on her first summer job; and Tanks, the brash loud-mouth dough-puller who was just working there until his big break as a rapper.

Tanks often sold mixtapes from his car; his driver-side door stood open as Melody pulled her car into the spot next to his.

He must be selling tapes to the customers again, she thought wryly as she reached out and slammed his car door. *He's going to get into trouble again -- why does he keep doing it?* Melody shook her head as she imagined Tanks being pulled into yet another meeting with Chris about his work performance. He had been warned that if it happened again, he might be let go and she hoped this wasn't going to be the breaking point. Truth be told, she had a little crush on Tanks and looked forward each day to just being in his presence. He never said much to her, but her heart smiled every time the fresh donuts got low and she got to walk over to him, look in his beautiful brown eyes and ask him to get more on the line.

There was another car in the parking lot that she didn't recognize -- must be a new employee -- she thought, as she rang the buzzer at the employee entrance in the back of the store. She waited for someone to peek at her through the little security window, but no one responded, so she kicked at the steel door. Luckily there was no time clock to punch, but she knew Chris would be watching to make sure she was at the counter at the start of her shift, and she didn't need this little delay to kick start a crappy shift at a crappy job.

She knocked this time, and her knuckles stung from contact with the steel door.

"Tanks! Jodi! Somebody open the door!"

She cursed and turned to walk to the front entrance when she heard the sound of the bolt being turned on the security door. When the door slowly opened, Tanks stood on the threshold, quietly staring at her.

"Took you long enough!" She yelled at him. "You trying to get me in trouble with Chris? I was knocking for-dam-ever!" She brushed past him roughly and hurried into the back room to put away her purse and grab an apron. Annoyed at having to wait outside so long, he didn't look so cute to her at the moment.

"Melody, wait," Tanks called behind her as she moved down the hall away from him.

"What is it? I don't have time for this --" she turned as Tanks was violently shoved forward. He stumbled and went down on his knees, catching Melody's eye with a look of fear that she had never seen before. She knew then that they were in real trouble.

She spun around to run into the manager's office when a leather-clad fist struck her in the center of her face with such force that she flew backwards against the wall before sliding down to the floor. The agonizing pain in her nose caused her eyes to water and blood gushed over her lips onto the front of her uniform. *Chris is gonna be so mad that my uniform is dirty.*

A shadow fell across her body as a large man stepped in front of her. She tried to look up at him but her vision was blurred from the pain shooting through her sinuses. The man bent down and grabbed the front of her shirt, and began dragging her into the office. She caught a glimpse of Tanks before she was pulled out of the hall; he was lying face down behind the door which he had held open for her moments earlier, a widening pool of dark red spread out around him as his life emptied from the opening in his throat.

Before she had time to grieve their unrequited love, she realized with a panic that she was going to be next, and she cried silently for all of the kisses they would never share. The darkness came fast for her; when she saw the blade of the knife bearing down, she closed her eyes and imagined she was standing in a pool of reds and blues and oranges, like all of the colors of the makeup kit she nearly owned.

"I'm the fucking best, if I tell you I got this, then I got this," Bruno Powell reached into his leather portfolio and removed a yellow legal pad to begin taking notes.

"Look, I'm going to be real honest with you right now. I'm one of the best criminal defense lawyers in the state – you lucked out by getting my name in the pro bono draw. I'm not even supposed to put in any work here, I'm supposed to just go through the motions and make it look good because I'm obligated to work a certain number of pro bono cases a year. You lucked the fuck out. And do you know why?"

Saul leaned back in the chair with his cuffed hands resting in his lap. He wasn't trying to hear the long speeches; he just wanted to know how he was going to get out of this one. With a record like his, it wasn't looking good for a dismissal. They've been trying to hang his ass since his first assault conviction when he was 15, and ten years later he was still managing to slip through their fingers, but this time, he was facing a murder rap. It was a different ballgame.

"No. Tell me why I should consider myself lucky," asked Saul.

"Because I'm not one of those pro-bono clowns who just do the minimum and keep up the appearance of *trying* to help you. I take every single one of my cases seriously – I treat every single one of my clients like you're my own family," Bruno leaned forward and stared intently into Saul's face.

"You, Saul, are like my own son. I have a son your age – his miserable ass mother took him with her in the divorce so I missed out on being there for his childhood. But you remind me of him, so I already have a soft spot for you. If you look me in the eye and tell me you didn't do this thing right here," He tapped his fingertips on the stack of papers on the table. "...if you're honestly telling me that you didn't do this, then I am going to make sure I get you home to your girlfriend in time for the birth of your baby."

"I already said I didn't do that shit," replied Saul. "This is some bogus shit. I went in there with Pancho to get his money from that dude that worked there; next thing I know, they fighting and this dude pulled out a knife and started trying to stab Pancho."

"But Saul, come on, you gotta work with me here – how did *everybody* in the donut shop end up dead? You're telling me that Pancho killed five people on his own?"

"I didn't do it, that's all I'm saying. I'm not trying to snitch on nobody and I can't tell you what he did because I wasn't looking at him - all I know is I didn't kill nobody!"

Bruno was furiously scribbling notes on the legal pad, nodding his head as Saul recounted the events of that night. This was going to be a tough one, considering that Saul was pulled over during a traffic stop and the police found a backpack in the trunk that contained bloody clothing, cash and jewelry belonging to the dead donut shop employees. Not to mention a knife containing DNA belonging to both Saul and at least one of the murder victims. The burden of proof was still on the State, but it wasn't looking too good for Saul in front of a jury. Unless Bruno could convince the jury that the entire crime belonged to Pancho, Saul's partner.

Pancho was a two-time loser with an arrest record as long as both legs, so it wouldn't be too hard to convince a jury that he was the mastermind behind the entire robbery, but how would he convince them that he actually killed five people, one at a time, without any help?

Bruno paused writing and rubbed his chin. It was going to be a challenge but not impossible. Nothing was impossible for the great Bruno Powell. His record was 0 for 250 - never lost a case, even the ones he did for free.

"Mr. Williams, let me get to work on this and start reviewing the materials. At first glance though, I can tell you that it's going to make me work! But like I told you – you got the right guy. I make miracles, baby!" Bruno extended his hand to Saul for a handshake; Saul hesitated not quite ready to trust, then slowly raised his hands to accept the gesture.

"Listen, take my card," Bruno stuck one of his business cards into

Saul's fingers. "If you want to call and give me some information I may have missed, call this number and either I answer or it goes to my private voicemail."

"I can't make phone calls, man, no money for the phone," said Saul.

"You can call your lawyer anytime for free," Bruno replied. "And if they give you any trouble about calling me, I want you to document it – names, dates, times – and let ME know!"

"So you really think I can beat this? My daughter is due in a few months and my girl really need some help."

"Brother, if what I've read so far is any indication of the case they have against you – I might even have you out in time to cut the cord." He raised his hand to count off the fingers. "We got illegal search and seizure. We got profiling – why did they pull you over in the first place? I'll tell you why, because you're a black man driving a nice car!"

"But it was a stolen car –"

"Did YOU steal it?"

"Nah, Pancho did."

"Well there you go, you didn't know it was stolen, and I'm already texting my assistant to pull the stolen car report and see when it was filed because I bet you dollars to donuts – no pun intended – that they didn't even know about the car being stolen when they pulled you over."

Bruno pulled his phone out of his pocket as he pushed back his chair and started arranging the papers to return to the briefcase.

"I'm also looking at how they mishandled the evidence - it was placed in the back of the police car! What kind of clowns are we dealing with here? That evidence wasn't secured, how do we know how the DNA got on it? You've got a criminal record, they could have planted your DNA on those things!"

He shook his head in disgust as he tapped out a text message to his assistant with a list of tasks.

"Saul, don't worry, I got this. We'll talk soon, Sir. I'm almost trembling with excitement to start ripping their case apart!"

And so he did. Each claim made by the prosecutor was swiftly and cleanly batted down by Bruno's objections; evidence was determined to be inconclusive and disallowed. The judge was disgusted at the level of sloppiness and the lack of organization by the State. They came to court expecting it to be a cakewalk and they were sent scurrying out of the courtroom, embarrassed and defeated.

The case against Saul was dropped for lack of evidence, and Saul walked out of the courtroom, a free man once again. Thanks to Bruno Powell, the system had worked once again, and he remained undefeated.

"I truly love my job," Bruno gushed to a reporter on his way out of the courtroom.

The only thing that Bruno didn't enjoy about his job was the pain he had to witness on the faces of the victim's families. That was always difficult.

He could feel their eyes boring into the back of his head, and he could hear their soft curses; wishing death upon him, his mother and even his unborn children. But he never let it sway him in his duty nor did he let their pain influence the way he doggedly pursued freedom and exoneration for his clients. He had a job to do and that's all it was, strictly business. He wasn't a monster, he was just doing his job and he happened to be damn good at it. After all, justice wasn't about whether or not you were guilty, it was about who had the best lawyer.

The fact was - whoever had Bruno Powell had the best lawyer.

When the judge announced that each of Saul's charges were dismissed, he began mentally preparing for the vitriol from the friends and families of the victims. He took deep controlled breaths and tried to relax before he turned to face them – it would be disrespectful to avoid their eyes and walk right past without acknowledging their hurt.

During every client's hearing, he would determine the leader of the victim's family and their location in the courtroom, so when he turned to leave, he could zero right in on that person's face, give a respectful and apologetic nod, and make his exit.

But on this day, the mother of one of Saul's victims stepped in front of him as he tried to scoot down the aisle behind the rest of his team. This case was unique in that there were five victims, and each of the victims had a mother in the courtroom, sniffling, sobbing and often wailing from the audience. His exit from this one would not be clean.

A woman stepped out of the row of seats and blocked his exit. She wore an oversized tee bearing a brightly colored screen-print of a young girl staring right into the camera. The words around her head said, "Rest in paradise, Melody."

Melody Davis. Bruno knew the name but had never seen the face. Well, not *this* face; not this soft round face with hazel eyes and pink, heart-shaped lips; a face so beautifully imperfect with a slightly crooked nose and a chin a little bit too long to be on a magazine cover. The look on her face as she gazed at the camera seemed to say, *'thank you for noticing me'*.

This wasn't the face that Bruno had known and associated with the name Melody Davis. The face he had seen in the crime scene photographs was bruised and battered with a boot print on the cheekbone where at least one of the defendants had kicked her in the face, likely while she struggled to hold in her guts as they escaped the gaping stab wounds in her stomach. The eyes that Bruno had seen were gray and cloudy from the absence of life; and the rosy pink lips were thin and pale from the absence of blood.

Bruno was still staring at Melody's image on the shirt when the woman raised her hand and took a swing at him. A security guard appeared and grabbed her hand mid-air while forcing her backward before she could make contact with Bruno's face.

"I hope you sleep well tonight!" The woman spat at him vehemently. "My baby's soul can't sleep because you just let the devil go free to kill again!"

The security guard signaled Bruno to continue his exit as he detained the woman. Bruno quickly mumbled his apologies, lowered his eyes and hurried through the doorway.

The woman screamed at his back, pushing against the outstretched arm of the security guard.

"You don't know the pain of losing a child! I wish you knew our pain!" She yelled as tears streamed down her face.

He tuned her out and reached in his pocket to put on his sunglasses. If he didn't shut down after the cases closed, he would never have any peace. He learned years ago to not take the cases home with him, leave the pain and the ugliness at the courtroom where it belonged.

The sunlight felt warm on his face as he stepped out into the parking lot, and a cool breeze passed by to dry the wetness forming around his eyes.

Bruno tossed and turned more than usual that night. He normally slept deeply in the king-sized down-filled mattress, feeling as if he was floating on a cloud. But on this night, sleep was not his friend. He turned off the television and closed his eyes, trying to think of pleasant things that made him smile, like the look on his partner's face when he told him that he'd won an acquittal in the latest case. His mind drifted to the boat that he was planning to buy; he could already feel the spray of water on his face as he navigated across the Detroit River. In his imagination, his son sat next to him the co-driver's seat as he pointed out the controls on the dashboard and asked if he wanted to take the wheel. Bruno Jr.'s eyes lit up and he stood to switch seats with his dad – when the boat suddenly lurched to the side and Bruno Jr. fell over into the water, screaming.

Bruno jumped up from his seat and tried unsuccessfully to catch his hand before he disappeared under the edge of the boat. He could hear the ominous thud as the boat bumped over his son's head.

Bruno woke with a jerk and a scream lodged in his throat. Shivering, he kicked off the damp sheets and every nerve in his body screamed at the shock of the cold air hitting his skin. He rolled out of bed, teeth chattering, and scooted across the wood floor to the robe hanging on the closet door.

He stood there in the dark, hugging himself and trying to generate some warmth from the robe and the friction of his hands. The dream had frightened him; he hadn't had a nightmare in a good many years, and this one was so vivid and terrifying. He picked up his cellphone and dialed the number to reach his son.

"Hey, Dad," a sleepy voice answered.

"Oh, hey, kiddo," Bruno relaxed and exhaled slowly at the sound of his son's voice.

"How 'ya doing, son?"

"I'm fine, I was sleeping – what's up, Dad?"

"Oh, nothing, I'm sorry, I didn't realize it was so late. I just wanted to chat a bit. I'll let you get back to sleep."

"Everything okay?"

"Sure! Sure thing! Everything's fine! I just woke up to take a leak and figured I'd call now before I got busy and forgot," Bruno looked at his right hand and saw that it was still shaking. He stuck it into the pocket of his robe.

When he was certain that Bruno Jr. was fine he ended the call and sat on the edge of the bed, thinking about his dream. It seemed so real that he could still hear the sound of the waves of water sloshing against the side of the boat.

In fact, it seemed as if the splashing water was coming from the master bath just a few steps away from the bed. *Had he left the water running before he fell asleep?* He pushed the bathroom door open and his eyes fell upon a young girl sitting in the claw-footed tub; her head hung down while her hands fanned the surface of the water. Her hair covered her face and he could barely see her eyes, but still he recognized her from the shirt.

"Melody," he whispered, hoping to break the spell and wake up back in his sweat-soaked bed.

The girl raised her head and looked at him with a bloodless face and eyes that had no pupils, but yet they stared and pierced straight to Bruno's soul. She stretched her lips across her teeth and gaped her mouth open into a soundless scream, so wide that he could see her uvula wiggle in the back of her throat.

Bruno had never met Melody. But he knew that she hated him, and that made his blood run cold when she placed each hand on the side of the tub and pushed herself up and out. Once she was standing straight, she lifted first one long pale grey leg out of the tub and then the other, moving slowly and deliberately in his direction.

"I'm still dreaming, I'm still dreaming." Bruno squeezed his eyes shut and shook his head to try to wake up but each time he reopened them, she was there still, swiftly advancing upon him.

He tried to run but he turned on his heels too quickly and his face hit the side of the bathroom door; pain shot through the bridge of his nose, momentarily blinding and defeating him. Cold, wet hands grabbed his face and pressed into his temples as they locked his head into place. Bruno's body trembled and he felt his bladder release, sending a warm rain down his cold legs and across his ankles.

The spectre resembling Melody came in close, tilting her head sideways with her thin white lips partly open, like a lover moving in for a sweet kiss – except this lover had cold clammy hands that felt like it had been pulled from the ocean. Bruno was helpless as he anticipated the touch of her lips on his, knowing they would feel just as cold and deadly.

She pressed her mouth on to his and he felt his knees give out at the same time as his bowels. He grabbed at her arms as he slid down the bathroom wall to the floor, but her hands wouldn't hold him; she stood and watched with dead eyes as he collapsed at her feet.

She knelt before him and began punching him in his stomach with her fists. To Bruno, her fists felt like the blade of a knife, even though he was helplessly watching her draw back for each punch.

Bruno opened his mouth to protest and beg for mercy but blood rushed over his lips, down his chin and flowed across his chest, pooling on the floor beneath him, before consciousness slipped away.

He spent a couple of weeks in the hospital; visitors came and went, standing around his bed looking worried and puzzled.

How could an intruder could slip into his home, stab him multiple times and slip back out without leaving a trace of evidence? Bruno couldn't explain it either, but he also couldn't tell them about the dead woman that appeared in his bathtub and proceeded to suck the air out of his lungs. So he stayed quiet and nodded his head agreeably when the detective questioned him; he simply answered the questions as vaguely as possible without raising any more suspicion.

His encounter with Melody haunted him, but he pushed it down each time it came to mind. He slept in the guest room for the first few nights of his return home, as if *she* couldn't find him in another room of the same house. He wanted to ask someone to stay with him, but he was afraid of appearing weak – he was *the* Bruno Powell! He was supposed to be fearless. He was on a first name basis with some of the most dangerous men to ever walk the face of the earth, how would it look if he asked someone to sleep over because he was afraid?

Bruno Jr. offered to leave school and come and stay with him for a while, but he couldn't take a chance on Melody hurting him, so he put on a most convincing act to change his son's mind and keep him far away.

He found peace for a while, but it was short-lived.

Nighttime was when he was most afraid, so he slept with the lights on and the bedroom door closed and locked. By the fifth night, he had learned to take his pain medication and sleeping pills together, allowing him to sleep deeply enough to avoid a late-night trip to the bathroom. It was with always with a sigh of relief that he would open his eyes to the daylight.

He woke up in complete darkness and his legs started shaking underneath the blanket. The clock on the nightstand indicated that it was just past midnight; he lay still and waited, knowing that *she* was near. The scene was set, the lights were off, and he could do nothing but wait for the show to begin. Tears welled up in his eyes – he was the most terrified as he had been in his entire life, and there was nothing he could do.

"Just kill me and get it over with!" He cried out into the darkness. "I can't take this anymore!"

Bruno knew she was there when the room grew ice cold.

"Please, leave me alone or kill me!" His body racked with his sobs as he cried like a baby, clutching the blanket to his chest.

He felt a weight on his midsection, pressing down as if something heavy was sitting on him. The air was forced out of his body until his lungs seared with pain – he needed to inhale but he couldn't expand – he was suffocating.

His body flooded with pain and his head felt ready to explode – if he wasn't able to breathe soon, he would either be brain-damaged, or he would die. He began to welcome death, anything to make the pain go away.

When the lights came on, Bruno opened his eyes and felt disappointed that he was indeed still alive. The sockets of his eyes were sore and throbbing, and his chest still ached from the pressure, but he was alive.

He curled up in a fetal position and cried for a while before getting out of bed to start the day.

"Whoa! First - what are you doing here? Second – you look like hell!" Kevin exclaimed when Bruno walked into the office wearing shades. Even on Bruno's brown skin the bruising was evident around the frames.

"Were you hanging from a tree all night, or what, buddy?" Kevin stood and approached him to get a closer look at Bruno's face.

"You got jokes, nice," said Bruno, brushing him away. "Don't worry about how I look. I'm ready to get back to work."

Bruno sat behind his desk and woke up his computer. He clicked through several screens until he found what he was looking for; minutes later, he was behind the wheel of his car, tapping an address into the GPS unit on the dashboard.

"Yo, Bruno, my man! What's up, dude?" Saul pulled Bruno into a tight hug, slapping him on the back as if they were old friends.

"Good to see you, Saul. I'm doing well, how are you?"

"I'm good man – but what about you, for real! I heard somebody ran up on you inside your house or some shit! What's up with that?" Saul waved Bruno inside of his small apartment and closed the door behind him.

Bruno removed his shades so Saul could see his face.

"Oh, shit!" Saul gasped. "How many dudes was it?"

Bruno replaced the shades.

"Yeah, yeah, good idea, put those back on!"

"Can I sit?" asked Bruno.

"Oh yeah, go ahead – wait, let me clean you off a spot," Saul began pushing aside the pile of laundry that occupied the sofa. He waved an invited hand toward Bruno when the spot was clean, then he pulled a chair from the dining table and sat across from Bruno.

"I'm surprised you came down here, slumming with us po' folks!"

Bruno laughed. "No problem. I had to make a stop over this way to pick up something from another client before I came here anyway. Not a big deal."

Cries from an infant came from another room.

"The baby? She's here, huh?" asked Bruno, extending his hand toward Saul to offer congratulations.

"Yeah, man, she came a little early," Saul grinned widely. "And I owe it all to you, man, for helping me be there for the whole thing. It was something else, man, like really wild."

"Did you cut the cord?"

"Aw, man, I didn't do all that, but I was there, that's my first born, had to be there. But that shit was wild! And get this – she already talking about trying for another one cuz she wanted a boy! Ain't that some shit?"

"Can I see her? Do you mind? I bet she's gorgeous – if she looks like her mom," Bruno joked.

Saul made his way to the back bedroom of the cluttered apartment, kicking shoes and baby items out of his path. He emerged a few minutes later, cradling the baby in his arms and cooing softly to her. Bruno had never seen him so gentle, the softness in his face when he looked at the child was difficult to reconcile with the man who was just facing charges for murdering five innocent people.

Saul leaned over and offered his precious bundle to Bruno.

"See, she don't look like my ugly ass, that's for sure!" He lingered a moment to make sure that Bruno was holding her securely before he pulled his hands away.

It was touching to see that he was capable of truly loving something, in spite of the gruesome evidence of his criminal history.

Bruno rocked the baby gently in his arms. It had been nearly 20 years since he'd held a baby. She smelled...well, she smelled the way babies smelled – innocent, sweet, a reminder of possibility of good in the world. He resisted the urge to lean in close and nuzzle her cheek.

"Name?"

"Zenobia Tamaris Alexander."

"Zenobia," Bruno repeated carefully. "Beautiful name."

"That's my girl's middle name and my mom's name," said Saul, proudly.

"So tell me something, Saul," Bruno asked, stroking Zenobia's face with his index finger.

"Your case is over now, no one can touch you, and I'm bound by client confidentiality so I can't do anything anyway – but tell me – did you kill those people at the donut shop?"

Saul looked at him with a blank face.

"What you bringing that shit up for?" He asked finally.

"Hey, it's just you and me – and Zenobia here, right? I just want to know, for my own curiosity. I mean, I know I'm good – I told you that when I first took your case. But with most of my clients, I always know whether they really did it or not. It doesn't change my commitment to defend you to the best of my ability, but I still *know* whether or not you did it."

"I told you I didn't do that shit."

"Yeah, I know, you told me – but that's what they all say. I think after what I did for you, the least you could do is tell me the truth."

Saul looked at the floor.

"Look, I....I didn't do all of that shit. Pancho started it, he cut the one guy's throat that opened the door, then after we had bagged up all of the money, he started telling me to go around and take off everybody's jewelry and get their cell phones."

"Right, right," Bruno nodded.

"Then the white guy got lose and ran in his office and tried to use the phone, so I had to stop him," Saul looked up at Saul. "I don't even really remember what happened after that, things just got crazy! Everybody started screaming and Pancho yelled at me that we had to take out everybody to shut them up. It just got crazy after that. I swear, I didn't do all of them, but I did a few, like two or three, just to make them shut up."

"Which ones," Bruno asked softly.

"What?"

"Do you remember which ones? Besides the white guy, that was the manager. Who else?"

"I don't know, man, I mean, I did the manager and both of them young girls because I couldn't do the old lady, she remind me too much of my moms."

Bruno smiled at Zenobia and bounced her gently in his arms.

"Do you feel better?" He asked Saul.

Saul smiled and laughed. "You know what – I do feel better! I feel like I just went to muthafukkin' confession!"

Bruno laughed as he reached one arm around to the back of his waistband and withdrew the burner he had borrowed from another client. Before Saul could react, Bruno placed the gun on Zenobia's forehead and pulled the trigger. His stomach lurched as her tiny head exploded in the blanket and splattered across his face and clothing.

Saul screamed and jumped out of his chair toward Bruno, then froze when Bruno pointed the gun at him.

"Hold it," Bruno said calmly, aiming precisely at Saul's head. "Don't move one inch."

Enraged, Saul gaped at the bloody remains of his baby girl in Bruno's grip.

"I just needed you to feel this for a second, the way the other parents felt," Bruno told him.

"I'm gonna tear your muthafukkin' heart out, man!"

"No, you're not," Bruno said softly before he pulled the trigger.

Night came and went, and Bruno didn't wake until he heard birds singing outside of his window.

After finishing his open cases (and even losing a few), he sold his half of the practice to his partner and retired his law license to teach at the University.

Over time, the bruises healed and he was eventually able to sleep with the lights off.

Foreword

My very first job out of high school was in the office of a rent-controlled, subsidized apartment building owned and operated by the city. In order to qualify for an apartment, you had to either be a senior citizen or on a disability status. The office manager was a bully who flew into irrational fits of rage whenever the tenants disappointed her by breaking something in their apartment – or paying the rent late. I've never forgotten about her, my first example of how NOT to be a boss.

Candace, this one is for you.

1st of the Month

GROANING LOUDLY, MK EASED her big body into the front seat of her grandmother's prized car. The springs of the car squealed as her weight caused the long-neglected automobile to shift on its chassis. The inside of the car smelled moldy and stale, causing MK to hold a hand over her nose to avoid inhaling the odor. She smiled as she looked around the car, taking it all in and wondering when she would get to actually drive her new possession.

"Could use some cleaning in here, first up," she murmured to no one in particular.

Her grandmother had been a heavy smoker, evident by the gray film covering the inside of the windows and the permanent layer of old cigarette smoke in the air. Nana was forced to stop driving her car years earlier when diabetes rendered her legs useless. Now, MK owned her very first car, and although it was ugly, rusted, out of style and smelled like death in a damp basement - to MK, it meant freedom, and she was going to clean it up, get it insured and *ride*. Well, maybe not all of that because it would cost too much - she was going to borrow a license plate from her friend LeRoy, slap it on the rear and *ride*.

MK adjusted the driver's seat and rolled her fingers around the steering wheel, thinking, *this is going to be nice. I'm finally winning!* Too bad she had to wait for Nana to die to get what she deserved, but Nana *was* old. Of course, it was tragic, but really - what was she hanging around for? Waiting to see her family grow up? Waiting to finish school and start a career? No, she had a good long run so it was time for her to move over and let someone else have her stuff. That someone would be her favorite great grandchild, Mary Kay, better known as MK.

She reached into her bag and pulled out her cellphone to text her best friend Dedra, letting her know that she had the keys to the car and would pick her up later. The old car would need a few hours of cleaning and airing out before she could drive; in addition, she still had to catch the building manager to see if she could take over Nana's lease.

She had truly hit the jackpot, she thought to herself as she danced in her seat. She deserved it, because riding that city bus was breaking her already tight pocketbook.

"Look what GOD did?" MK shouted happily, thinking about how blessed and favored she was.

She exited the car and shut the door, placing the keys in her pocket. She needed to work fast because the morgue wagon would soon arrive to pick up Nana's body, and she wanted to catch the manager before he made any important decisions.

MK breathed heavily as she pumped her fat legs across the tenant parking lot toward the building entrance. An old black man sat in the foyer with his wheelchair facing the wall, and MK resisted the urge to grab the handles and turn him around so he could at least look out onto the sidewalk, but he seemed content to stare at the wall. He looked as if someone was in the process of taking him from the building and began turning his chair to ease it out the door, then got distracted and left him sitting there. He didn't seem to mind, he had either found something fascinating on the wall or he was totally oblivious to his surroundings. MK looked back at him as she passed and saw that both of his feet were wrapped thickly with gauze that was long overdue for changing.

Entering the lobby, MK was slapped in the face with the strong smell of pine cleaner and a freshly mopped floor leading to an unmanned receptionist's desk. She approached the desk and waited for someone to acknowledge her presence. She looked around impatiently for assistance while drumming her fingers on the wooden ledge.

A door opened and in shuffled an elderly black woman, pushing her walker ahead of her frail body. The aluminum walker clattered against the door frame as she emerged from behind, gripping the bars with hands encased in long white ballroom gloves. MK smiled as she recalled how her Nana's hands were always cold and she would often wear gloves throughout the day, something about her age and poor blood circulation kept her feeling cold.

"Can I help you?" The old lady rattled her way over to the desk and collapsed in the chair, letting out a deep sigh as she sat.

"I'm Emma Randolph's granddaughter. I need to see the building manager, please." Speaking her Nana's name caused sadness to wash over her; saying it now made it all feel so final – she was really gone.

The woman squinted at her through eye lashes tinged in gray, and worked her mouth furiously, making chewing motions like a rabbit. MK suddenly realized that she was wiggling her loose dentures around with her tongue.

"Ms. Randolph? Ms. Randolph gone, baby. She ain't here no more," said the woman.

MK sighed. "Yes, I know, I'm the one who found her this morning, now I need to take care of her apartment."

"Did you talk to Mr. Rhodint?"

"Who?"

"Mr. Rhodint, he runs this place," replied the woman.

"That's what I'm asking you for now, to see if I can talk to him," MK rolled her eyes and tried to mask her agitation. As much as she loved old people, they could also really work her nerves like no one else.

The old woman shook her head as if she were just as annoyed with MK. Her bony hand pushed a wig curl behind her right ear and MK could see that her ear was missing the full earlobe; the remaining skin looked ragged and *chewed*. MK took a step to one side so she could sneak a look at the woman's left ear, but the lobe on that ear protruded beneath the edge of the wig so she could see that it was intact. She shuddered a bit at the idea of an earlobe being snatched off in some freak accident. The vision of the lobe tearing from the ear caused her to inadvertently reach for and stroke her own earlobe as if to reassure herself that it was still there.

"Look, please, ma'am, I don't mean to be any trouble. I just want to talk to the manager before he makes any plans for my grandmother's place," pleaded MK.

The wrinkled jaws started working again, sliding the denture plates back and forth. This was her thinking mode, MK realized, so she fell silent and waited for the woman to deliver the results of her analysis.

"She ain't been dead long enough for the water to get hot! Ain't it too soon for you to be worried about that?" The woman replied after a few moments, clearly, she disapproved of MK's mission.

A softer approach is needed, MK thought. It was important that she win this battle, no matter how much shit she had to eat, she was going to get that apartment to go along with her car. She had no other hope of getting off of Dedra's couch and into a place of her own.

She took a deep breath and leaned on the counter with the biggest smile she could muster under the circumstances.

"Ma'am, I'm so sorry - I didn't get your name?"

"They call me Miss Jackie."

"Oh, *you're* Miss Jackie?" said MK, slapping her forehead dramatically. "I should have known it was you! My Nana used to tell me all the time about how hard you worked down here, trying to keep everything running smoothly!"

"I most certainly do," replied the woman as she tucked the wig behind her ear again.

"I know you do, my Nana always said, Miss Jackie should be the building manager because she does everything around here!" MK shook her head. "So I finally get to meet the Miss Jackie that I've heard so much about!"

Miss Jackie had begun moving things around on her little desk, picking them up and putting them down in a different spot, trying to look busy. She was eating up the praise, just as MK intended.

"Miss Jackie, I am just still so shaken up from finding my Nana this morning, so I apologize for being a pain to you right now. I will get out of your hair as quick as I can! Lord knows you don't need anything else on your plate!"

Miss Jackie's face began to soften.

"Okay, baby, I'm gonna let you go and talk to Mr. Rhodint - but don't you be wasting his time with foolishness. He's a business man and he don't like to be bothered 'less it's important!"

MK raised her palm. "I promise, Miss Jackie - no foolishness!"

"Take the elevator, go down two floors; his office is at the end of the hallway," Miss Jackie reached out with her gloved hand and smacked the hidden buzzer underneath the ledge on her side.

A loud ring signaled access to the residential hallway and MK grabbed her bag and rushed forward before she could change her mind.

"Thank you, Miss Jackie!" MK yelled over her shoulder as she disappeared between the doors. Once the doors closed behind her, she had to stop and lean against the wall to catch her breath; she silently vowed that she was going to start exercising and lose some weight after she got settled into her new place. It was hard to take proper care when she was living out of a garbage bag and sleeping on a broken down sofa.

MK headed down the long hallway. As she passed doorways, she could hear movement behind the doors; the rustling and swishing sound of bodies pressed against the opposite sides of the door - maybe peering through the peepholes? She heard the unmistakable clicks of door locks being turned amidst feeble coughs from the occupants.

"What is with these folks? Think I'm gonna break in or something?" MK snorted and pushed the down button on the elevator panel. While waiting on the elevator to arrive at her floor, she snorted at the crudely written signs taped to the wall that entertained her whenever she visited.

Notify the Building Manager if you are going on vacation.

Pay your rent on time and you'll be fine.

Contact Management in case of financial issues.

The elevator announced itself with an orchestra of screeches and pops; MK hesitated before stepping into the doors. She was still chuckling at the ominous warnings of the signs when the doors separated to allow her entry. Another handwritten sign hung on the back wall that said simply, *Have you paid your rent this month?*

MK laughed and pushed the button for the Basement. The elevator churned and tossed, causing her to grip the rails for the short ride. When it stopped with a bump, the doors slowly crawled apart and MK stepped out and turned to walk the hallway toward the manager's office. A bright red arrow was -hand painted on the wall to direct her to the end of the corridor.

He couldn't be more hidden if he tried. His office was situated at the very end of the long dim hallway peppered with light fixtures that were either completely bulb-less or the bulbs had blown out. There were only two lights flickering to illuminate the path to the Manager's office. If those two lights burned out, the hallway would be in complete darkness. Being in that part of the building gave MK a feeling of uneasiness; she wondered how often the elderly and disabled tenants made the unsettling journey down into the basement, if ever.

There were no apartments on the basement level, only doors marked for various utilities and storage, and a few unmarked mystery doors. The last door bore a simple nameplate with the word *Manager* engraved on the surface.

MK approached the door hesitantly and took a deep breath before knocking. A raspy voice granted her permission to enter and she turned the knob and pushed against the heavy door. Thick smoke floated out into the hallway and caused her eyes to burn as she stepped across the threshold. She rubbed her eyes and fanned at the smoke in her face, clearing a visual path to the desk in front of her - and there he sat. The man for which she came: the Manager, Mr. Rhodint.

She saw his stomach before she saw him: the big fat belly was clearly running the show, a large portion of it sat up on the desk and the rest of it was pushed down out of sight – but you knew it was there just below the desktop; he was without a doubt the fattest man MK had ever encountered.

Wow, he's bigger than me! She thought as she took it all in. She didn't immediately see his face because his neck and head seemed to disappear down into his shoulders, but when the smoke cleared and he saw her standing in front of him, his head popped up from the folds of fat around his neck. His eyes were wide and round behind wire-rimmed glasses, darting nervously around the office and behind MK, as if he were frightened of being caught with her in his office. He wiggled his nose nervously as if he were sniffing the air. MK felt herself shrinking – which wasn't easy for a big girl - as he sized her up.

"*Clothe* the door!" He barked at her with a gruff voice. "Hurry, *clothe* the door!"

MK reached back and pushed the door closed, sealing herself in the smoke-filled room with the strange man with the lisp.

She stayed close to the door to keep the distance between the two of them, although she was certain that if he tried anything, she'd be out of the door and down the hall before he could uncork his girth from the chair. She could run when she had to – she had been chased by a store manager a few weeks earlier when she was boosting, and she out-ran him with ease. She thought her lungs were going to explode when she finally stopped but it was mostly the hard edges of the iPod boxes in her bra.

The room had no air vents; it seemed to be a storage room that he had converted into an office, and she wondered how he could stand working in such a dim and sour space without any fresh air.

He didn't move from the desk. He sat and stared at her with beady eyes in a face like whole wheat dough. A handful of tight naps scattered across his mostly bald and sweaty head, and the room smelled like bologna that had been left out of the fridge too long.

He spoke again and snapped MK out of her thoughts.

"Can I help you, *Mith*?" MK was fascinated with the way he spoke. He was a complete package of jokes, tied up with a little ribbon on top; the appearance, the smell, and now, a lisp. She couldn't wait to finish her business down here and call her friends to share. She briefly wondered if she could maneuver her phone out of her pocket and secretly record just a few minutes of this hilarity.

"Yes, I'm Mary Kay - are you the manager?

"Might be. Might be not? Who want to know?"

MK stepped closer and stuck out her hand. "Sir, my grandmother is a tenant here – *was* a tenant here until this morning. I would like to take over her apartment."

"Who *ith* your grandmother?" He grunted, ignoring her outstretched hand. He moved a big meaty paw to pull open the desk drawer and retrieve the accounts ledger. Flipping it open, he began rifling through the cards.

"Ms. Randolph, she passed away this morning and I wanted to see if I could take her place over and continue paying her rent so you wouldn't have to go through the trouble of finding another tenant. I can move in today, if you want!"

"I don't *thee* her in here," he said after a few minutes of searching.

MK nervously cleared her throat. "Maybe you moved her to another file since she - you know - passed away?"

He looked up at her then, examining her face, then slowly dropped his eyes down her front until he reached her feet, where he stuck his tongue out of his mouth and licked his puffy lips. MK wondered what he was thinking as he surveyed her large body. She thought she saw a quiver rip through his body and it made her feel dirty; she pulled her sweater together and held it closed with one hand.

"You might be right. I think I put her in the *other* file," he pulled out the desk drawer on the opposite side and removed a small stack of cards held together by a rubber band.

"Ah, here it *ith*. Emma Randolph. I remember her well. I'm *tho thorry* for your *loth*."

MK cleared her throat and tried to ignore the giggles that were trying to work their way up to her throat.

"Thank you, Mr. Rhodint. What do I have to do to take over her place? I'm sure you want someone in there to keep the rent up."

"*Thath* important. I don't want to *looth* rent on the unit. Do you have a job?"

"Yes, I work at the Shop 'N Save just a few blocks from here," MK lied, not wanting to admit that she was unemployed. But she just needed to get into the apartment and she'd figure out how to pay the rent after she got settled in.

"This would be so much closer to work for me too, I wouldn't have to spend an hour on the bus every day commuting to the store."

Mr. Rhodint rubbed his chin and continued to size her up with his beady eyes.

"I run a very tight *thip*, Mary Kay."

"MK, everyone calls me MK," she smiled and tried to warm him up; he was such an odd fish – or maybe that was odd whale in his case - it was difficult to tell in which direction the conversation was heading.

"MK. *Thith* apartment building hath 100% *occupanthy becauth* I take care of my *tenanth*. I don't put up with people moving in here trying to *dithrupt* the *peath* and quiet. Moth of my *tenanth* are mature, *dithabled*, retired, or people who want to *ekape* the *thitty* life."

"I'm sorry – did you say, the *shitty* life?"

"*Thitty! Thitty* life! Not country, *thitty*!"

"Ohhhh, okay, I'm sorry, *city* life."

MK was overwhelmed with trying to suppress the laughter and decipher what he was saying because it seemed like it was very important – but his lisp made it difficult to focus or take him seriously.

"I understand completely. That's what I'm looking for, someplace quiet. I don't cause any trouble, I just go to work and come home and read." She giggled inside. Read? She hadn't read in quite a while, but if she got a nice little apartment of her own, she was sure she could find a book to read.

"Rent *ith* $500 a month. Due on the *firth*. No exception. No *excuthes*. No *grayth* period. No late *feeth*. *Juth* don't be late. I don't *akthept* late *paymenth*," said the manager.

"That won't be a problem, Mr. Rhodint," replied MK..

He looked over the card in his hand and then raised his head to MK.

"You're lucky, your *grandmotherth* rent *ith* already paid for the month, you won't have to pay for two more week. But I will need a *thecurity depotith* to let you move in."

"But isn't there already a security deposit on the place? I mean, from my grandmother?" MK asked.

"Yeth, but that her *depotith*. You need to put one up *yourthelf*, to *thecure* the apartment."

"Well, that's going to make it a little more difficult for me," said MK, dropping her head to look at her shoes.

"Mary Kay, I have found that people *apprethiate* thing more when they have *thomething* to *looth*. If I *juth* let you move in without putting up any of your own money, you have nothing to *looth* and you have no *reathon* to care," he tossed the cards back in the drawer and slammed it shut, effectively dismissing her.

"Wait, wait, I mean, I can get the money but it might take me a little while to put it together, and in the meantime, you're going to have to clean out her place, advertise that its available, interview people - all things that are going to cost you money and time. You may not even have it rented again in time to make next month's rent, or the month after!"

Mr. Rhodint rested his hands on the desk and looked MK up and down again before speaking.

"I *thuppoth* you're right," he conceded, removing an application packet from a letter tray and sliding it toward her along with an inkpen.

"*Thave* me trouble, *thave* me money. I will keep the *depothit* I have and let you move in. But *pleath underthand* my *ruth* - no late rent. And no *noith*."

MK picked up the ink pen and reached for the papers when Mr. Rhodint placed his hand on top of the paper and pressed down tightly.

"Never," he said, making eye contact with her over the top of his glasses. "My *ruth* are not negotiable. If you want to live here, you follow the *ruth*."

"I get it, thank you, you won't regret your decision," MK smiled nervously and he released the papers. *Just follow the ruth.* She snickered quietly.

"Take *theeth* with you, read them and bring them back *thigned*."

"Oh, no, I'll sign them now. I'm sure it's just the standard leasing stuff. I'll sign so I can start getting settled," MK began flipping through the pages and scribbling her name on the signature lines on the bottom of each page.

"If you're *thure* that what you want to do," Mr. Rhodint replied, leaning back in his chair and wiggling his nose as he watched her sign each page without reading any of the words other than Sign Here. She was going to be a fun one, he thought, just what the building needed -

fresh meat. The others were getting so old and unpleasant.

"*Nith* having you join *uth*, Mary Kay," he said, taking the papers from her hand. "*Thee* you on the *firth* of the month."

MK was tingling with excitement and could hardly wait to get on the other side of the door and start doing a happy dance. She barely heard Mr. Rhodint's last words as she rushed out of his office. She just wanted to get out of that miserable space, back down the hall and up on the floors with daylight, fresh air and people that didn't smell like greasy meat.

MK entered the apartment quietly, instinctively looking around the living room. She almost called out her Nana's name out of habit, and felt a lump in her throat when she realized that she would never again hear a response to her call. There was no indication that the morgue had collected the body, so she wasn't surprised when she entered the bedroom and saw her Nana still lying on the bed.

She sat next to her and looked into her still face. Nana lay on her back staring up at the ceiling with her mouth hanging open as if she had uttered a final word, perhaps an "ahhhh" as she met her Maker.

Well, it wasn't quite an *ahhhh*, it was more like an *ummmph* as MK held the pillow over her face. At least that's what it sounded like as she pressed down until she thought she might crack the woman's fragile old skull.

I should close her eyes, thought MK. Poor thing looks like she's about to open a birthday present. *No more birthdays for you, Nana. You've had plenty.*

She pushed and pulled at one of Nana's eyelids until she got it to slide over the dry eyeball, but it kept snapping back open. She was disappointed in herself for not thinking to close the lids before rigor mortis set in, but she was in a hurry to get it over with. She had waited for months for the perfect opportunity and there was always something in the way – a visit from a neighbor or a phone call from a chatty member of her knitting club. All the while, MK waited and plotted, until she finally arrived and caught her sleeping; no distractions or interruptions, it was time to make her move.

She heard the sound of a siren approaching the building so she blew Nana a quick kiss and left the apartment to greet the medical technicians in the hallway. While she leaned against the wall and waited, she cried softly as she remembered her Nana.

The technicians had finally removed Nana's body and MK set about airing out the place by opening the windows. Over the years, people had given Nana candles as gifts, but she never lit them because she was afraid that she might set the place on fire. MK found the stash of candles on the shelf of the coat closet and looked around for a fire source. The stove had electric burners so it was of no use; she decided to ask the one-eyed neighbor for a lighter or book of matches.

She stepped next door and knocked, waiting for the sound of footsteps on the other side.

The man in the connecting apartment opened his door to peek one eye out through the security chain.

"Who's there?" The voice sounded frightened.

"Um, sir, it's me, I'm Ms. Randolph's granddaughter? Next door?" MK added, rolling her eyes.

"What do you want?" he whispered tersely through the crack in the door. As he moved his head, MK could see that he had a patch on the other eye, and he must not have been wearing it long enough to adjust to it, because he kept putting it up to the slit in the door as if he had forgotten that he couldn't see through the patch.

"I just wanted to borrow some matches, or a lighter, if you have either," replied MK.

After assessing the level of danger, he then pulled his working eye away from the door, closed it and clicked the lock as if he thought MK might try to get into his home next. She could hear the security chain being slid across the latch. "Weirdo," she mumbled, and turned to go back inside of her apartment when she heard the neighbor's door crack open again.

"Here!" He stuck out a long thin pale arm and shook a cigarette lighter at her. "Take it, hurry!"

In two steps, MK was wrapping her fat hand around the lighter.

"Thank you, sir," she said, before he slammed the door.

She spent the rest of the day cleaning and dusting and stripping down the bed where Nana took her last breath. She felt a twinge of sadness as she moved about the apartment removing remnants of Nana. The ceramic nativity scene went into a box; the wax fruit from the bowl on the dining table went into the trash: everything had meaning and memories, therefore, it had to go because she didn't want the bad *juju*.

Back and forth, she stacked the boxes in the hallway for a maintenance worker to carry downstairs to the storage area. By nightfall, she was too tired to make the walk to catch the last bus, so she decided to sleep there and retrieve her things in the morning. Maybe she'd take a chance and drive the old car across town, it should be okay, as long as the cops didn't get behind her.

It felt glorious to run a hot bath and submerge her body in the bubbles. She soaked until the water turned cold and the skin on her fingers and toes wrinkled; then she refilled the tub and soaked some more.

When she finally stepped out and dried off, she forced her arms into Nana's robe which she found hanging on the back of the bathroom door. The sash barely wrapped around her waist and she tied the ends in a little bow to close the front, then slid between the fresh crisp sheets with a tear in her eye at her fortune.

She fell soundly asleep as soon as her head sank into the pillow.

Piercing screams ripped into her wall of sleep. Her eyes popped open in the type of panic that grips your chest and squeezes your windpipe. Lying still, MK held her breath and looked around the room in the darkness. Nothing but shadows bounced off the walls from the tree branches outside of her fourth floor window. When it became apparent that a branch was scraping against the glass, she relaxed a bit, convincing herself that the branch must be the culprit.

"Stop it, girl," MK laughed nervously to herself. "We don't have to be scared no more!"

She watched the branch drag across the window again before she felt her nerves releasing their death grip. The sheets were drenched in sweat so she kicked the top layer off of her legs and let the cool breeze flow across her and dry the sweat.

It's just a tree branch. MK thought, and slowly released her breath through tight lips. She rolled to the side of the bed and put her feet on the floor, feeling around for the slippers that Nana kept next to the bed. They must have been kicked away during the commotion surrounding her dead body, because they weren't in their usual place.

MK slid down to the floor to look under the bed and heard the scream once more. This time, she was wide awake and kneeling, with her head almost touching the floor, so there was no mistaking what she'd heard. It was coming from the apartment on other side of the wall – *the man with one-eye.*

It started out as a low moan, building steadily in pitch, becoming a blood-curdling garble. MK froze, afraid to move even an inch, fearing that her weight would cause the floor to squeak and attract the attention of whomever – or whatever - was inflicting the agony next door.

She listened to the man cry, "Please, no more, please, I'm sorry! Give me another chance!"

She wanted to grab her cell phone and call for help, but she couldn't move - surely someone else had to be dialing 911 to save this poor man. There was no way that she was the only person listening to her neighbor possibly being slaughtered on the other side of the wall!

Another nerve-jarring scream shook the wall and then an accompanying silence that was just as chilling as the scream. MK half-rose from the floor and leaned across the bed; trembling and dripping sweat from both panic and discomfort. The walls were so thin that she could hear a grotesque squishing and grunting sound: squishing, like someone walking on freshly soaked carpet – but the grunting, try as she might, she couldn't work out a plausible scenario for the grunting.

She stayed on her knees in that praying position until daylight started to invade the room. Her legs had locked painfully into position and her gown was now soaked in urine – but it was morning and the sound of life in the building gave her the strength she needed to pull herself up from the floor.

The irony was not missed that she'd moved miles away from the hood but was still spending nights on the floor in fear.

"So, you're in, huh? I can't believe you pulled it off!" Dedra squealed into the phone.

"Girl, yeah, three weeks now - loving my new place! I gotta redecorate though because it's all *old* up in here," replied MK as she walked around the apartment taking mental notes of the things she wanted to change or replace.

"You should have a housewarming party!"

"Hmm, I don't know, I can't really have parties up in here, it's not that kind of place."

"Come on! That way people will bring you new stuff for your place!" exclaimed Dedra.

"I wish I could but I gotta keep it really low key; this place is quiet and they don't like parties and shit. I can't be getting kicked out as soon as I got here!"

"Pffft!" Dedra sucked her teeth. "Come on, what are you scared of? You're gonna start changing on us already?"

MK could feel herself getting annoyed. Dedra was always so pushy and MK didn't like being bullied into doing things she didn't want to do. Their friendship had been like that since childhood; Dedra would come up with crazy ideas and coerce MK into going along, then MK would be the one to get into trouble for it because Dedra was a tiny cute little thing and MK was the not so cute, overweight friend.

"I don't know, I just don't want to mess up," MK could already feel herself starting to soften.

"Okay, then how about I just come over with pizza and drinks and we'll have a little quiet get-together? We have to celebrate some kind of way!" Dedra begged, but she was already planning the party because she knew MK would go along with it.

"Just you - and maybe a couple more. I don't have that much furniture in here yet so about four of us will fill this room up," conceded MK after a moment. "Let's do it tomorrow night."

They ended the call and MK stood looking around the apartment with a smile. A small get-together was just what she needed to shake from her head the sound of those horrifying screams.

She was still confused about the events of the previous night, but when she heard movement in the hallway, she raced to the door to see a young man exiting her neighbor's apartment.

"Hey!" she yelled, stepping out into the hallway before he could disappear.

He stopped and turned around but didn't move any closer.

"Is he okay?" MK asked, nodding her head toward her neighbor's door.

"Yes, I just came by to pay his rent - I'm his nephew," replied the man, his eyes darting around nervously.

The neighbor poked his head out into the hall – the most MK had seen of him since she moved in. He nodded toward his nephew, signaling him to hurry along; as he started to pull back into his apartment, MK saw that the arm holding the door open was bandaged and in a sling.

He met MK's eyes one last lingering moment before he closed the door. MK shrugged and decided to mind her own business.

"If he likes it, I love it!" she said aloud. "I'm surely not going to waste my time worrying about somebody that ain't worried about their damn self."

She went back into her apartment, then stopped to yell out the door, "I'm not gonna take being woken up from my sleep too many more times either!"

Just as she settled into the couch to relax, a knock came at the door and she threw up her hands, agitated at the interruption.

"So you decided you wanna be friendly now?"

She stomped to the door and rose up on the ball of her foot to look through the peephole, expecting to see the neighbor, but instead she saw the top of Mr. Rhodint's balding head pressed close against the viewer.

She drew back in disgust and quietly lifted her hand from the doorknob, placing it on the side of the doorjamb to steady herself as she watched him. He knocked again and she stood frozen, breath caught in her chest.

Why is he here? Rent isn't due for another week - what on earth did this vile man want?

The door cracked with the strain of Mr. Rhodint's body pressing against it; MK leaned forward slowly to look again through the peephole. He was standing so close to the door that she could barely see him, pushing in as if he was listening for her movement. She was repulsed at the idea that the two-inch thick wooden door was the only thing between them, keeping him from being fully fused into her body like a layer of skin.

"Mary Kay."

MK's blood ran cold at the sound of his voice coming through the seal of the door.

"Mary Kay. The rent is due *thoon*. *Pleath* don't be late."

MK didn't speak or move. The hairs rose on the back of her neck and she imagined his lips pressed against the crack of the door, leaving wet imprints as he spoke.

His breathing was ragged and she could smell his breath as it seeped through the door, that same sour odor from his office, like room temperature salami; and then the sound of him pulling – no - *peeling* himself away from the door with a soft wet pop.

He abruptly took a step back and stared at the door, as if he *knew* she was right there, close to him, watching. His body was wider than the entrance and he seemed to be trembling – *pulsating* – as he stared, waiting for her to make a sound.

She didn't. She was good at pretending not to be home, she'd played that game many times with bill collectors and other people she'd owed money.

He doesn't know who he's messing with. She thought, and then cringed as she watched a dark shadow fall across his face. His eyebrows wrinkled behind his glasses and he scowled at the door before turning away.

MK was only able to exhale when the coast was clear and she rested her forehead on the door. She would have to lay low for a while until she could pay the rent.

Follow the ruth.

She tried to tiptoe quietly back to the sofa, where she sat for a long time trying to stop the shaking.

The music was bumping, the liquor was flowing and the tiny apartment was pulsating with bodies moving and grooving to the heavy bass.

MK was frantic. Besides the fact that her "small get together" had turned into a gathering of many; every time she turned the music down, someone would increase the volume until the stereo was again bouncing off the walls.

"This is NOT cool, Dedra! I can't have all of these people in here! How did they even find out?"

"I don't know, girl. Just relax and enjoy your party," Dedra said, as she waved her off with a flick of her hand.

"Relax? I can't relax, you guys are going to get me kicked out! I can't have parties in here!" MK surveyed the room of gyrating bodies, trying to identify the faces as they danced back and forth past the kitchen counter.

There must have been at least 35 people standing, sitting and kneeling around the two room apartment. Some were huddled in conversation around the sitting area; some leaned against the walls, nodding their heads and observing, and a few had boldly taken up residence in the bedroom, lounging on her bed and watching a movie.

MK had no idea how it had gotten so out of control. Dedra showed up with pizza, drinks, their friend LeRoy and his girlfriend. A short time later, Dedra began smirking as she repeatedly tapped on her cellphone to respond to notifications, then she made the announcement that their friend Tyler had arrived and wanted to be buzzed up. From that point, it seemed the party-goers multiplied in the blink of an eye.

"Dedra, what if the neighbors report me?"

"Stop worrying! You're entitled to a housewarming! What kind of place doesn't want you to have a housewarming? Here, get me more --" Dedra shoved her empty glass toward MK and flipped her ponytail.

"I'll be right back - I see something I wanna get into." She began two-stepping away from MK and into the crowd of dancers.

MK stared angrily at Dedra's back as she left her standing there; she was not going to let her friend ruin her only chance at a normal life. Nana's passing was both a tragedy and a blessing, and here was Dedra trying to mess it up by bringing her hoodrat attitude across town into MK's new life. No, that just won't do. She loved Dedra like a sister but damned if she was going to allow that to keep her from moving up in the world.

'Dedra!" She tried to yell over the music and wave her hand to get Dedra's attention. Her friend had made it across the room and was now grinding against a man MK had never seen before. The man ran his hands up and down the front of Dedra's body; she leaned her head back on his shoulder and closed her eyes as they bopped and swayed to the music. MK knew that Dedra could hear her calling above the din of the party because she raised her head and looked around briefly with glazed eyes; she heard her, she just didn't care.

"Bitch!" MK turned and picked up Dedra's glass, excusing herself as she forced her way through the crowd to get into her own kitchen. Dedra hadn't specified what she wanted in her glass, so she slammed it down on the counter and surveyed the assortment of liquor bottles that had collected on the sink.

She was rolling her neck around to relax the tension in her shoulders when she noticed the neat row of prescription bottles lining the back of the drinkware cabinet. She opened the door and reached over the glasses to grab a handful of the bottles. She recognized the painkillers that Nana used to take after she lost her leg. At 1200mg each, they were a powerful dosage. Nana must have been in some serious pain in her last days and MK felt a twinge of regret at not being there for her.

She filled Dedra's glass with the tequila and then opened her palm over the glass and allowed a few of the pills to sink to the bottom. She stuck in a finger and stirred until the powder disappeared from the surface.

"Coming through again, excuse me please!" She maneuvered her way through the crowd until she was standing in front of an already mellow Dedra.

"Here, you didn't say what you wanted so I just poured tequila," she thrust the glass toward her friend, who took it eagerly and turned it up without question. "I figured you'd drink anything."

Dedra emptied the glass and handed it back to MK. "Hey, MK, meet Shawn. Shawn, this is my bestie, say hi," she commanded. Shawn man leered at MK and fixed his stoned eyes on her chest.

MK took the glass and stepped back to lean against the wall, watching as

Dedra returned to groping and grinding against her partner. He looked over Dedra's shoulder and winked at MK, making her stomach churn. She knew what that wink meant; it meant that Dedra had been whispering in his ear, making him promises that included the use of MK's bed after the party. But MK wasn't going to play along this time. She had a new life and she'd decided tonight that Dedra just didn't fit into it.

She watched until Dedra hit the floor, stepping forward just in time to catch her before her head struck the cocktail table.

Shawn helped carry Dedra to the bedroom and shoo away the rude guests lounging there. Together, they stretched her across the bed and covered her with a throw blanket. They removed Dedra's shoes and Shawn's hand lingered a bit too long when it brushed across MK's arm, but she shot him a look making it clear that she was not going to be pinch hitting for her drunk friend.

"Can you help me get rid of these people?" MK asked him, batting her eyes. Perhaps a little flirtation would ensure his full cooperation. "I think my girl here really needs some peace and quiet because she's going to have a helluva hangover when she wakes!"

"Sure, sure, let me go and clear out everybody," Shawn said as he left the room. MK could hear his deep voice rumbling through the apartment amid a chorus of rising protests and the sound of the door opening and closing rapidly as they disbursed.

MK sat on the bed and listened to Dedra moan and stir. She was trying to come out from under the fog but the pills in her system kept sucking her back down. MK tenderly stroked her friend's arm, then leaned over and whispered in her ear.

"It's okay, buddy, I know you're feeling weird right now, but it's just the stuff I gave you. Don't worry, I'm right here. I'm not going anywhere."

Dedra whimpered and tried to pull her arm away but MK tightened her grip, squeezing so hard that Dedra's skin turned deep red beneath her fingers.

"Just be still, it'll be over soon," MK whispered again, stroking the length of her arm.

She waited until it sounded as if the peace had been restored to her apartment before peeking out of the bedroom door. Shawn was heading back toward her and she stopped him.

"Is she okay?" He asked.

"Sure she is, she just can't hold her liquor sometimes. Been like this since we were teenagers. I got her, don't worry. You can leave now," MK told him.

He looked disappointed and he just stood there staring at her for more direction or promise, until she spoke again. "I'll make sure she calls you in the morning, okay?

His face brightened then. "Okay, I'll be waiting."

MK watched until he left the apartment before she stepped out to look around and make sure she and Dedra were alone. She locked the door and stopped first in the coat closet and then the kitchen, to gather some items before returning to the bedroom.

Dedra had managed to roll over and was trying to drag her limp body off the bed but her bones were like noodles and refused to cooperate; her upper half hung over the edge of the bed and her cheek was resting on the floor. The ponytail she'd pinned in the top of her head was now on the floor next to the bed, as if she'd ripped it out in frustration.

MK sighed and scolded her. "My pretty Dedra, why are you straining yourself? You can't get away. You're just making it worse, you silly girl!"

She dropped the stack of garbage bags she held under her armpit and approached the bed, grabbing Dedra's foot and using it to pull her back up on the bed. She climbed on top of the mattress and rolled Dedra on her stomach, then threw her leg across her back and mounted her, sitting her full weight on Dedra's lower back.

Dedra exhaled sharply as her breath left her lungs, feeling the bulk of MK pressing the air out of her stomach.

"Can't...breathe..." Dedra gasped weakly.

"Don't worry about it, hun, you won't need to breathe much longer anyway," MK had wrapped a leather belt around both fists, and she threw it around Dedra's head, roughly snatching her backwards by the throat. She pulled both ends of the belt tightly as Dedra choked and gagged for air; she managed to drag her hands up to her throat where she clawed at the belt cutting into her windpipe, but it was no use. MK was bigger and stronger, and Dedra's will to live had already been severely altered by the painkillers and alcohol in her system.

MK was drooling as she watched the back of Dedra's head bob up and down with the force of her tightening the belt. How much longer? Her mind wandered as she thought about what she had to do next and she wanted Dedra to just give up so she could move this along.

Her arms started trembling as she grew weary of holding such a tight grip on the belt; just when she was ready to quit, she felt a soft rumble between her thighs as Dedra's life ended, and she heard a soft dull pop from Dedra's neck finally broke, giving in to the belt.

MK leaned forward, panting and dripping sweat on the back of Dedra's head. She chuckled as she thought about how angry Dedra would be at her hair right now – ponytail on the floor, hair loose and sweaty, just a complete mess!

Now for the real work.

She climbed off of Dedra's back and leaned over to look in her face. Her eyes were not only wide open but they were bulging from the sockets. MK shivered started to remove all of her own clothing first, then Dedra's. She put on the safety glasses she'd found underneath the sink, then picked up the electric knife.

As she made the first cut through the meat and hit the bone, she prayed that she had enough garbage bags for the job.

If I keep cleaning like this, I'll lose weight in no time!

MK giggled as she knelt on her hands and knees and scrubbed at the bloodstains next to the bed.

There was more than she'd estimated but it wasn't so bad. It took several trips down to the dumpster to dispose of the bags but other than MK nearly having a heart attack, the execution was almost surgical.

She squeezed the bloody sponge into the mop bucket and wiped across the area once more before calling it quits. Pulling herself up, she groaned at the pains shooting through her body. She was going to need another soak before she could turn in for the night or else she would wake up *stiff as a board*, as Nana used to say.

MK danced around the kitchen, snapping her fingers and waving her arms in the air to the music playing through her cellphone. It was delivery day for her furniture from the Rent-to-Own store and she was feeling ecstatic. Laid out on the counter was a sheet of lined paper on which she had sketched a layout of her new living room to show exactly where each item of furniture would sit. Every few minutes, she would dance her way over to the paper, study it, then pick up the pencil lying next to it and make changes to the details.

She had found a small velvet drawstring bag in the cushion of Nana's old sofa and after sorting through the crumpled dollar bills and coins, she had close to $100, enough to make a down-payment on the rent-to-own contract for the furniture and a few groceries to hold her over until she could pawn Nana's jewelry. She soaked the old furniture with fabric refresher and let it air out before selling it to a friend. It wasn't much to look at but three rooms of old people furniture for $75 was a deal that nobody could pass up.

Soon, she would have the place looking and smelling like there was life inside, instead of the stale gray existence that had been Nana's world.

She had yet to find a job but it wasn't for lack of trying. She had put in applications everywhere but nothing had come through for her yet, throwing a kink in her plans because rent was now a week overdue and she'd been using the back entrance to the building for the last few days, hoping to dodge any known informants for the manager.

I just have to make it another week or two, then I know I'll find something and pay the rent, better late than never!

A knock at the door shook her from her daydreams. It must be the furniture! She rushed to the door and wrapped her fist around the knob to open it, then squealed and drew her hand back in pain; the knob was glowing red and the skin on her palm was already red and blistering, like the time she accidentally leaned back on the electric stove and put both hands flat on the burner.

MK cried out in agony as she rushed to the sink to submerge her hand in warm water. Her legs trembled and tears rushed down her cheeks but the water offered slight relief from the searing pain. Her mind was racing, was the building on fire? Why didn't she hear any fire alarms or sirens?

"Mary Kay."

MK soaked a towel in water and wrapped it around her hand before turning off the faucet.

"What do you want?" She yelled, wincing at the pain.

"Mary Kay, I've been more than pay-tent with you. You are not following the ruth. I warned you not to be late with the rent."

"I got your rent! But I'm not gonna be treated like this! I'll give it to you tomorrow! Go away!" She screamed at the door.

Her hand throbbed painfully as blisters formed across the surface. The door squeaked and whined and she turned and stared at it as it yawned and seemed to bend inward on it hinges. MK didn't know how long the wood would hold him out and she began rummaging through the drawers with her one good hand, pushing aside silverware in search of something sharper, deadlier, something that would help protect her from him...or, it...whatever it had become. She didn't know, but she was very afraid as her hand closed around a big butcher knife and she immediately raised it in the air, defensively.

"Mary Kay! Don't make thith hard. Open the door."

"Go away!" She screamed, fighting tears. "Leave before I call the police!"

He laughed. A macabre laugh that came from deep inside of his throat, full of dark undertones and threatening promises; MK knew it wasn't gleeful laughter -- it was the sound of him preparing to come in and take what he came for.

The pressure on the door suddenly stopped and it seemed to straighten as he moved away. MK grabbed her cellphone from the counter and quickly dialed 9-1-1, then pressed the phone tightly to her ear while holding the knife out in front of her.

"Please answer, please please please!" She cried into the mouthpiece, sinking down to the floor with her back against the stove.

"We're sorry, your call cannot be completed as dialed. Please hang up and try your call again."

"Noooooo!" MK screamed and pressed Redial, only to hear the same message.

"MK."

A key was pushed in the lock and the doorknob began slowly turning until he pushed at the door and the security chain stopped his entry. MK moved faster than she had in a long time as she crawled through the kitchen, knife clattering across the floor, and made it into the bedroom just as she heard the security chain pop and the door burst open, slamming into the wall behind it.

She felt his presence behind her in a split-second, amazingly fast for a man of his size, and her mind hadn't begun to process the probability of him crossing the room that quickly before he grabbed her leg. MK screamed and flipped over to slash at him with the knife, but when she faced the threat, what she saw made her stop screaming and instead wither in unparalled fear.

Mr. Rhodint – what appeared to be Mr. Rhodint through the peephole – was completely unrecognizable as he loomed over MK and fixed glowing red eyes on her face. His body had morphed into a lumpy mass of throbbing flesh; short misshapen arms jutted out of his side, and the huge hands were tipped with long black claws. His skin was glistening with sweat, beaded across a fine layer of short black fur, and as he leaned over her foot, his mouth came open with a soft pop and that's when MK caught the glimpse of his sharp teeth sliding down from the top of his mouth.

She was riveted by the sickly yellow fluid that oozed out of his mouth and covered her foot – until the searing agony reached her nerve center and made her snap out of the spell. He was holding her foot so tightly that she couldn't move her body without twisting her ankle, but whatever was dripping from his mouth was burning through her skin on contact, the way acid burns through a Styrofoam cup, her skin sizzling and falling away from the bone like it had been cooked all day in a boiling pot of water.

She was too deeply shocked to scream, and too deeply wounded to fight; the room spun around her at dizzying speed and she could barely make out the sight - and sound - of Mr. Rhodint chewing away at her foot. Her limp body shook like a rag doll with every tear of his teeth at her flesh.

After a while, it didn't hurt anymore. She just stopped feeling altogether. Before the room went black, she wondered how long before he made his way up to her plump thigh.

MK rolled out of bed and gingerly touched her foot to the floor, testing the tolerance for the pressure. The foot still responded with a considerable amount of pain, so she would need her painkillers to get moving for the day. She felt sad to realize that she wasn't quite ready to forego the crutches.

She opened the pill bottle on the nightstand and popped a couple of the caplets into her mouth, washing them down with the glass of water she kept next to the bed.

As much as she wanted to stay in bed, she needed to get moving – albeit slowly – to catch the bus downtown to the Center for the Disabled and apply for a job she could do while sitting; perhaps as a receptionist or toll-booth clerk. A neighbor has given her the info and assured her that they would be able to put her to work quickly, even with her disability.

Hobbling slowly to the window on the crutches, she drew back the curtains and stood looking out at the parking area beneath her window. Her little gray car still sat in its spot, waiting for someone to show it some love and put it back on the road, but driving was going to be a long way off for her, if at all. The prosthetic foot her doctor ordered would not be ready for at least two months, and then she was going to need rehabilitation classes to learn how to walk with the device before trusting herself behind the wheel of a car.

Perhaps she would be better off trying to sell it to come up with the rent for next month.

Foreword

It's always easy to write about demonic kids. Think about it, they make perfect little monsters in a nice, compact package – easier to pick up and throw when necessary, but hard as hell to shake if they get their teeth locked into your leg. Above all, they're usually always hungry, even when not possessed by evil forces.

Playground

RUNNING AS FAST AS his legs would carry him, Mykal cleared the field of the playground and crossed over into the bordering acreage. He spotted a wide leafy bush and dove headfirst behind it, hitting the ground and stretching out low so he could scoot beneath the low-hanging branches.

Luckily, he was wearing his favorite black jeans and a black tee shirt – perfect for hiding in the dirt! No one would find him now! He covered his mouth so his giggles wouldn't give away his location.

He could hear the other kids running and laughing, some screaming in the distance, as everyone hustled to find the perfect hiding spot. It took all he had within him to not give himself away as he watched gymshoe-clad feet run past him, frantically searching. No one else would think to dive underneath the bush but he was the best at Tag because he wasn't afraid to squeeze himself into tight, dirty or dark places. Other kids wouldn't go into the basement of an abandoned house, up a tree, or climb over in a garbage dumpster – heck, once he hit behind a DOG.

That particular day, he was getting tired of running but knew he couldn't use any of his previous spots; he was about to give up hope until he realized that he was near the backyard of his friend Topher, and Topher had a big hairy German Shepherd in the backyard – a dog that happened to love Mykal! Why didn't he think of that sooner? He quickly leaped over the fence and coaxed the dog to lie down next to him while he scratched the side of his coat facing away from the fence.

The other kids ran past and didn't even see him stretched out next to the dog; the dog didn't bark or move as long as Mykal kept scratching.

He became a legend that day.

Under the bush, things had gotten quiet, so he rested his head on his folded arms, he might even take a short nap. When all of the others were tagged, he could come out the winner once again. He peeked through his arms and saw one of the girls ducking down behind the trunk of a tree about a yard away.

What a stupid idea! They'll find you real quick there!

She tried to hug herself closer to the tree but she was wearing a white blouse so Mykal guessed she would be eliminated shortly, and he was right.

He watched as Timothy walked up behind the girl and tapped her on the shoulder. She jumped and fell backward on the ground, laughing.

"You got me, Timothy," she said through her smile. "I'm glad because I'm hungry and I'm ready to go home anyway."

Timothy stood over her smiling. Then he knelt down on his knees, grabbed her face with both hands and sunk his teeth into her throat, ripping and tearing at the skin while her hands flailed and slapped at his head. Mykal didn't understand what he was seeing; he wanted to climb out from under the bush and run across the grass to get a closer look because it wasn't registering in his brain – did Timothy just kiss her neck? Or was he really tearing a hole in her throat? That couldn't be because then she would be dead – right?

And if she was dead, then why was she getting up off of the ground and walking around looking dazed and bloody?

Timothy wandered away with blood running down his chin and the girl stumbled about in circles until another child ran past her and tapped her on the shoulder, screaming, "You can't get me!"

She raised her head and started propelling her body in the direction that child had gone. Mykal kept staring, afraid to move. Screams rose and fell across the playground – some were laughing, but some were blood-curdling; you couldn't tell much of a difference unless you listened closely – or unless you had actually witnessed someone having their throat partially eaten by another child.

He lay as still as he could, listening to the screams, trying to decipher whether or not he recognized any of the voices. If he did know them, they sounded pretty different now that they were no longer living.

His crotch grew warm as his bladder let loose, and the ground beneath him became soaked, but he would not move, could not move, could not even breathe.

His Auntie would be looking for him soon.

Night turned into day and Mykal was still lying under the bush, watching as the other kids ambled across the field toward the houses, walking slowly with an awkward crooked gait; their heads cocked sideways as if they were using sound to direct them home.

They had started the evening in clean, fresh play clothing, and they were returning home soaked in blood and entrails, wearing the blank wordless masks of the undead.

Mykal watched them cross the field and disperse toward their separate homes before he slipped out from under the bush and took off running toward his own home. The early morning wind was cold and sharp in his face and felt like ice in his lungs, but he didn't stop until his hands closed around the brass knob of his own door.

"Lawd ha' mercy, you're alive!" Auntie Bee threw up her hands and screamed with joy when he burst into the house. "Praise the lawd, praise the lawd!"

She grabbed him and kissed all over his head and face before her tone changed.

"What the hell is wrong with you, making me worry like that!!! I should whip your ass!"

Mykal didn't have time for pleasantries. He turned the bolts on the front door and ran to each window, flipping the latches as he ducked beneath the ledge.

"Boy, what are you doing?" His aunt stood in the middle of the floor with her hands on her hips. "I need some answers right now! Where the hell you been all night? I called some of your friends and a couple of them were gone too – now I understand if you want to camp out or something, but –"

"Auntie Bee, please...*shhhhhh!*" Mykal touched his fingers to his lips. He was being disrespectful and ordinarily this would earn him a sound slap across the mouth, but this was no time for manners. The screams were starting to circulate through the courtyard, and pretty soon, the horror would reach their doorstep.

Mykal figured they had ten minutes at best to get in the car and speed away from the subdivision faster than any of the dead could travel. If they could get to the sheriff's station at the next exit off the highway, they could warn them and maybe call in the National Guard and whoever else you call when it's too big for the local law. But he would need Auntie Bee to move fast – and the only time she moved fast was when she was running late for church. This was the exact *opposite* of church.

"Auntie Bee, I'm sorry, but I need you to listen to me very carefully," Mykal pleaded as he wrapped his arms around her waist.

"I'm sorry I stayed out all night but I really need you to listen to me right now, Auntie Bee. There's something *really really* bad happening outside and we have to get out of here right now!"

"What on earth are you talking about, Mykal? What kind of bad things?" She asked, pulling him away from her body so she could look down into his face.

"I don't have time to explain everything, just please trust me," Mykal held up his finger again and whispered. "Listen....do you hear that?"

The screaming. It was much louder now. And much closer. Not just screams but moans and deep gut-wrenching growls that conquered up images of something so utterly menacing and blood-thirsty that it had to come from the pits of Hell. Auntie Bee's eyes widened as she realized what she was hearing – she was very familiar with things crawling out of the pits of Hell because she'd studied her bible for 62 years, waiting for this moment.

Mykal snapped her back to attention. "Do you hear it, Auntie Bee?"

She nodded.

"We need to go. *Now*. Where are your car keys – in your purse?"

She didn't answer.

"Auntie!"

"No...no...hanging on the nail in the kitchen," She was afraid and Mykal didn't expect that. After all, she had told him his entire life that when the end of the world came, she would know exactly what to do and he should not be afraid because she had always anointed him in the blood of Jesus. He was not prepared for her to be weak right now, he needed her to drive them away from there. If this was truly the end of the world then he was going to fight until the lights went out!

"Stay here, Auntie – *don't move!* I'll be right back, we're going to get in the car and drive really fast, got that?"

She nodded again.

"Don't move. Wait, get your purse and that's it. You need your purse."

Mykal left her standing in the middle of the floor with one hand clutching her shirt collar and the other balled up in the folds of her skirt as if she was trying to restrain herself from hitting something.

He looked at the nail hanging by the fridge – nothing. Mykal sighed, of course the keys wouldn't be exactly where she said, they never are. He began pulling out each counter drawer and rifling through to see if she had dropped the keys inside in a moment of absent-mindedness. His panic was building as he reached the last drawer and still no keys. His eyes were drawn to the coats hanging on the rack near the back door and he rushed over to search the pockets.

As his hands closed around the keys deep inside the pocket of a raincoat, voices rose from the living room and his heart sank. Auntie Bee was babbling, then screaming, until the screams were cut short by gurgling, as someone – or something – had begun to attack.

He couldn't just leave her. He had to at least *try* to fight for her! The block of knives sat in their usual place on the counter next to the stove; he grabbed the knife with the biggest blade and longest handle, pulling it cleanly out of its wooden slot. His knees trembled as he tiptoed to the living room, gripping the knife in his fist, warrior mode with the blade pointed downward.

It was already too late. A little girl he didn't recognize straddled Auntie Bee's thighs and tore away at her midsection, pulling and ripping at her insides as she fed them into her mouth like bloody frankfurters. The girl's eyes were closed; her head thrown back and what was left of her face pointed to the ceiling.

Auntie Bee was gone but Mykal had no time to mourn. The front door was standing wide open and he could see other kids walking aimlessly around outside, kids that looked just like the little girl feasting on his Auntie, bloody and lifeless. He knew it was only a matter of time before more of them were inside of his house to join the buffet so he had to act quickly.

Stepping carefully toward her, Mykal raised the knife in a wide angle across his chest before bringing it down with all of the strength his ten year old body could muster – cleanly separating the already-dead girl's head from her neck.

A boy with long bloody dreads stepped across the doorway and headed toward Mykal. Turning on the balls of his feet, Mykal ran through the kitchen and out the back door.

He ran across the field, his feet occasionally slipping on the grass still wet from fresh morning dew. Pumping his arms and legs, he tilted his head back away from the wind, the way his gym teacher taught. The cold air whipped around his face, drying his eyes and drowning out the cries of pain and anguish behind him.

He wanted to get to the one place that he knew would be safe. It had all started there, so he knew they wouldn't come back, and he could hide high in the top of the spiral slide, just until the danger was over.

The big knife in his fist nicked his side each time his elbow cut through the air, but he wouldn't stop running – he couldn't stop running, not until he reached the playground.

Three months before the thing that happened.

"So this is your big idea, huh?"

"Yep."

"You're not scared of getting caught?"

"Nope," George swept his eyes around the dark field looking for movement, but it was still and quiet and nothing moved but the wind in the trees.

"Stop bitching and get your suit on," He ordered Stanley, his partner. They walked to the back of the truck and pulled the protective outfits out of the bags. George picked up a spray container and aimed the nozzle at Stanley, signaling him to turn around so he could disinfect his clothing. Stanley covered his face and spun in a circle while George covered every inch of him with the protective chemical, then offered him the hose so he could repeat the task for George.

Wordlessly, they pulled the long yellow gloves up their arms to the elbows, then shrugged the jumpsuits over their shoulders. The boots and helmets went last, flipping the clear plastic eye shield down and giving the thumbs up sign that they were ready for the main course.

Beneath a tarp secured by bungee cord were twelve 250 gallon tanks, labeled with the image of a skull and the words, DANGER, DIOXIDE.

The men moved from tank to tank, carefully disconnecting the safety caps and removing the pins to ready them for disposal. George attached the industrial spray system to the first tank and bumped Stanley to move back as he aimed at the field and prepared to release the chemical.

It rushed through the rubber hose and sprayed 50 feet into the air, falling like a fine mist across the soil and disappearing into the ground.

The men continued emptying the tanks, watching the gauges drop and skillfully moving from one to the next until the dozen tanks were empty.

With their task complete, they cautiously doffed their jumpsuits and repeated the decontamination process before climbing back into the front of the truck.

"If this hits the fan, I don't know nothing about it," Stanley said nervously.

"I already know."

"Make sure you do! I mean it, I wasn't here!"

George rolled his eyes and snorted.

"You tell me this every time we come here," said George. "What's funny is that you don't mind splitting the cash but you wanna turn pussy when it's time to do the work!"

"I just don't like it – but I got bills to pay like everybody else. But if this ever gets out, we're all going down. And I bet we'll get stuck with all of the charges because we won't have big fancy lawyers like the dude that owns the company!"

"Look, nobody is paying attention. After the gas explosion over there –" George nodded his head in the direction of the burned out homes standing a few yards away. "- they're too busy settling lawsuits to worry about the dirt over here!"

Stanley's eyes started to water and he wiped at one of them with the back of his hand.

"If you say so, just remember – I was never here with you."

George put the truck into gear and drove slowly away from the abandoned playground with the lights off.

Foreword

One of the things I love about road trips is the long stretches of smooth road where you don't have to hit your brakes. One of the things I hate about road trips are the miles and miles of cornstalks on the side of the road; so thick that you wouldn't be able to hit your brakes fast enough if something stumbled out into your path.

If I'm not driving, I won't sleep; I keep my eyes peeled along the crop line, ready to shout out a warning if I see any movement. Just don't expect me to stop and offer my assistance.

Ride

END OF SHIFT – the best part of the job. If you made it to the bottom half of the clock with all of your limbs and no brand new holes in your body, then you had a great day.

Officer Rick Petty was having a damn great day. The body count was unusually low for a weekend; weekends were usually when the local natives grew restless and tried to kill each other for entertainment purposes.

Missing his regular bounty of speeding tickets and seatbelt violations, he managed to peel off a satisfying amount of hours sitting off the highway, behind the wheel of his cruiser; eating and looking at porn on his cell phone. Every now and then, he'd get a call to assist another officer by securing evidence or helping to hold back the inconsolable relatives of the victim. But the majority of his twelve hours on the clock that day were full of the usual quick and easy tickets for things like burned out tailgate bulbs, or whatever he could come up with.

His favorites were the out-of-towners. It was always fun to convince them to pay immediately for any violation he decided would get him the most cash. That little trick sometimes earned him as much as an extra $500 per day. Yes, the out-of-towners were the best!

It wasn't that he wanted to do such things, but he needed every dime to pay his miserable shrew of an ex-wife, *may that bitch burn in hell!* She wouldn't be happy until he was living in a cardboard box on the side of the freeway, begging for change. She would never forgive him for – according to her – screwing up her life, as if he and only he were responsible for her destiny.

Well, soon, she would get what she'd been asking for. He knew people, he had connections, people that owed him, people that he'd arrested in the past for some very bad things. He didn't want to do it, he'd warned her, but she kept pushing. So he was going to push back.

The radio interrupted his thoughts, crackling and hissing at him,.

"RP – we got a call about a little girl wandering in the road. Are you able to take it? It's out near you, I think."

Rick sighed and thought about it a moment before answering.

"Alright, I was about to wrap it up for the night but I'll check it out on my way in."

"Got it. The caller said she was just walking with no shoes on and he tried to give her a ride but she ran into the crops."

"In the crops?"

"That's what they said, in the crops at the Turner Corn Field!"

"Okay, I'll pass by there in a few minutes. Out."

He drove until he reached the Turner farm, then pulled off the road and drove slowly along the crop line; his tires crunching as they rolled over dead, dry stalks lying on the grass.

When he reached the end of the field, he turned around in the road and drove along on the opposite side, turning on his floodlights to illuminate the darkness.

"There ain't shit out here," he said to himself. "I'm done, waste of my fucking time." He reached for the radio on his shoulder to report, when something stepped in front of the car and he bumped it before he could slam on the brakes. He felt the hood make contact before it went to the ground.

"Oh, shit, oh, shit, oh, shit!" He threw the car into PARK and hopped out, holding his flashlight in one hand and pushing the button on the radio with the other.

The top of her head barely cleared the front bumper; thick black curls spilled out on the ground and he could see just a hint of a bloody forehead.

"Just hold on, sweetheart, I'm gonna help you!" He punched the radio button again but only received static as a response.

"Officer needs help!" He panted into the speaker.

The girl moaned and moved her head slightly, enough to reassure him that she was alive, at least. Rick dropped to his knees next to her and looked to see if she was snagged in the underbody.

"It's okay, sweetheart, I'm going to get you out – are you hurt anywhere?" He asked.

She shook her head.

"Are you sure?"

She stretched so her face was fully visible, and Rick was immediately struck by the intensity of her eyes; they were deep and dark like pools of ink, and he felt an unease looking into them. Guilt, perhaps, from hitting her with the car, even though she had stepped out in front of him so quickly, there was really nothing he could have done. After all, it was now dark outside – why didn't *she* see *him*? What the hell was she doing out there anyway?

"I'm sure," the girl said, locking her eyes into his until he looked away.

"Okay, if you're absolutely sure, I can pull you out, but I want to make sure nothing is wrong so I don't make it worse. Okay?"

"Okay," she replied.

Rick crouched at her head and grabbed under her armpits, then gently pulled back until her little body cleared the vehicle.

She sat up and crossed her legs, then started shaking her thick curly hair with her hands, removing the dirt and grass.

"Thank you," she said, and stretched out her hand for Rick to help her to her feet.

"What are you doing out here? Are you lost? The nearest house is still a couple of miles away!"

"My name is Nika," she said casually. "What's yours?

"Officer Petty, nice to meet you, Nika," Rick pushed the button on the radio and waited for a response but it had gone silent. "Hold on, let me get this call in, something's wrong with my gear."

He walked around to the car door and leaned in to use the stationary radio. The screen on the display was black and all of the activity lights were off.

He chuckled. "Okay, must be some malfunction, I'm gonna have to take you to the station so I can use the phone."

Nika shrugged. "Whatever, Officer. I got nothing but time."

Rick waved his hand to the opposite side of the car and Nikka walked to the back door and climbed in.

"Why are you getting in the back – are you a criminal?"

"No. Are you?"

Rick regarded Nika in the rearview mirror. She was so small but so confident at the same time; he guessed that she was at least 7 or 8 years old, but she had an eerie sense of calm that belied her young age.

She sat in the back with her legs crossed underneath the skirt of her thin, dirty white dress. She was barefoot, just as the caller reported, and streaks of dried mud decorated her arms and legs. A wild tangle of matted hair framed her sweet, innocent face, but her eyes told a different story.

She raised her head and met his eyes in the mirror and he looked off into the cornfield as he drove.

"*Are* you?" She repeated.

Rick chuckled.

"I'm the good guy, Nika! Didn't your mommy teach you that? That cops are the good guys?"

"My mommy doesn't like cops," Nika replied.

"Well, that's not nice," Rick stretched and yawned.

"You're not nice either," Nika said, shrugging her shoulders.

Rick had met these types of smart-assed little kids before. It was pretty common in his line of work. Little criminals in training, he called them. He would arrest their parents for drugs, shoplifting, disorderly conduct; and their offspring would run up to him and beat on his legs, crying and demanding that he let their parents go. Sometimes they would bite and kick him and he'd be tempted to take the handle of his gun and pop them upside the head; knock them out for a while, that would teach them to defy an officer of the law!

"Why don't you come sit up here? Only bad guys sit in the back. I'm not arresting you – yet!" Rick snickered at her.

Nika pulled herself over the back of the seat and flipped into the passenger side with ease, dutifully snapping the seatbelt across her waist.

"So tell me – how did you get out here?" Rick asked when she settled in and resumed staring out the window.

"How did *you* get out here?" Nika responded.

"Um, it's my job, I patrol this area."

"I never see you patrolling."

"You've seen me before?"

"Of course. I see you all the time."

Nika danced her fingers along the console, tracing the stitching in the leather. Her fingernails had been chewed to the quick and the cuticles were dirty and ragged.

"So you live out here? You're not lost – you stay out this way?" Rick eased his foot down on the brake. If the little brat lived nearby, there was no need to waste time going to the station and working overtime on paperwork when he could just drop her ass off at home!

"I live wherever I want to live." Nika turned to him and grinned. Her teeth were tiny and chipped in places; clearly she wasn't on a first name basis with a dentist.

"Okay, enough with the games, I will pull over and put your ass out."

"It's dark out – you won't do that, you'll lose your job."

Rick swerved off the road and aggressively slammed the car into PARK.

"Look, I don't know what kind of game you're playing but I'm technically off work right now! I don't have to put up with this! I can easily radio for someone else to come and get you and I can go home."

Nika tilted head and squinted her eyes.

"You can't do that – your radio isn't working. Look –" She pointed at the black panel.

"Maybe I can't call anybody, but I can put you out and leave you. Obviously, you don't need help, you just want to play games. That's what I'll tell my sergeant. Or..." Rick crossed his arms. "...or I'll just pretend like I never saw you."

"What if something happens to me out there?"

"Not my problem, we never met."

Nika threw back her head and laughed.

"Okay, okay, I'm just messing with you, Officer Rick! Keep going, take me to the station. I'm hungry now."

Rick shook his head and slowly pulled back onto the road.

He hadn't seen another car for quite a while. Unusual for that stretch of the highway – it was dark and mostly uninhabited by business or homestead, but there was a busy shopping center several miles away and traffic flowed back and forth from either direction.

They rode in silence until Nika sneezed.

"Bless you," said Rick.

"Don't bless me."

"Why not?"

"You don't have that much power. Do you?"

Rick rolled his eyes. "I have to say, you are the strangest kid I've ever met. Who gets offended at someone saying, bless you?"

"Do you believe in Heaven, *Officer Rick*?"

"What? Of course. Why – you don't?"

Nika shook her head, then leaned over and put her face close to the dark computer display. Rick thought for a moment that the screen tried to flicker and come to life, but nothing changed.

"There's no heaven or hell. It's only blank out there."

"Blank?"

"Blank. Like this computer. Just blank. Darkness. You turn off, like someone took out your batteries."

"Damn, you're a weird one," said Rick. "I bet you're a riot on the schoolyard."

"Do you have kids, *Officer Rick*?"

"No, no kids. No wife either."

"Hm, I thought you had a wife," Nika was looking at him again, he could feel her eyes on the side of his face. She made him nervous and he felt the urge to move his service pistol from within her reach. *But she's only a little girl.* Still, she made him nervous.

"I'm divorced, not that you need to know – you won't tell me anything about yourself, so why should I tell you about my life?"

"I know everything about you already."

It occurred to Rick that this girl must be part of the roaming gypsies that came to town every year and set up camp on the farthest part of town. They put up tents and danced and sang, then wandered around begging for donations. After a month or so, they'd pack up and disappear. They were real slick, they tried all kinds of tricks to make you believe they were magic, pretending to read minds, cure your diseases, all the while picking your pockets.

Very funny, he knew her game. She'd had him fooled for a short while but now he got it. He decided to play along.

"What do you know about me, Nika? Astound me with your mind-reading skills, why don't you?"

She was drawing a picture in the slight condensation of her window.

"Tell me about your baby."

"Wrong - I don't have a baby, I just told you I didn't have any kids."

"I know you don't *now*. You killed her."

The tires left black marks in the pavement as Rick snatched the car off the road, running the front end into the row of stalks.

"Get out!" He screamed at her, spit flying from his mouth and landing on the passenger side window.

Nika smiled at him sweetly. "What's wrong, *Officer Rick*?" She had a disturbing way of saying his name that sent chills up his spine. He didn't know who this child was – or *what* she was, but he wanted her away from him.

"Get out, now!" He screamed again.

Nika crossed her arms and stared straight ahead, refusing to move.

Rick opened his door and marched around to the passenger side, snatching her door open and grabbing her arm.

Pulling her out, he threw her to the ground a little harder than he'd planned but he wasn't going to apologize.

"Walk your ass home – whoever you are! Good fucking luck too!"

He got back in the car and pulled away quickly, glancing briefly to make sure she still standing there. She waved at him cheerfully. Rick bit his lip as he took in the image of the stick family drawing she'd made in her window – a man, a woman, and a little girl.

His heart was pounding so hard in his chest that he started taking deep breaths, rolling down the window to get fresh air; rolling down the passenger side window to erase the stick figures. Beads of sweat popped out of his forehead; he was angry – and scared.

How dare she?

"I didn't kill her!" He yelled out loud. "I didn't kill her!"

Cristela.

He hadn't said her name in years because he wanted to forget. He had been so tired that evening after working a long shift, and that nagging bitch insisted that he bathe her. He told her he was too tired, but she didn't care. He *told* her that he could barely keep his eyes open, but she laughed at him and called him weak.

"I can push a damn baby out of my vagina and your punk ass can't stay awake long enough to rub some soap on it? Are you fucking kidding me?" She yelled at him.

It wasn't his fault. He tried, but she was so slippery...and he was *so tired*.

Everyone agreed that it wasn't his fault. So who was this kid to come along and throw it in his face? *Who was she anyway?*

"I bet she's a relative of that bitch!" He said, angrily. "She probably set this up, trying to set ME up, make me get put on a psychological eval, lose my job!"

"How you gonna get your alimony if I lose my job, stupid bitch!" He laughed hysterically.

"It didn't work! It didn't work! I'm on to you!"

He almost didn't see Nika when she stepped in front of the patrol car. He screamed and lost control as the steering wheel jerked out of his hands. The car whipped off the blacktop and ran into the stalks at high speed; coming to a stop when the front end dipped and slammed into a mound of dirt.

The airbag activated, exploding from the center of the steering wheel and punching Rick backwards with such force that his nose ran blood down his lips and chin. He struggled to unlock his seatbelt but the impact of the crash caused the belt to tighten – for his own protection. The airbag was holding him firmly in place against the back of the seat. He felt along the side of his seat until his fingers closed on a switchblade he had confiscated earlier from a juvenile; with a flick of his wrist, he managed to stab at the airbag and loosen the pressure.

Nika was on top of the hood, kicking with her feet and beating with her fists, screaming his name.

"Officer Rick! Officer Rick – come out here, let's talk some more – I won't bite, I promise!"

He felt fear in his veins. Fear of a little girl. And he just wanted to get his hands on his gun so he could feel safe again. His positioning in the seat wedged the gun too tightly between his thigh and the console, and there wasn't enough room to maneuver it from the holster.

Nika grew quiet and the pounding on the hood stopped; he reached for the driver side door handle and pumped it once to open. Rolling out and hitting the ground, he quickly contemplated taking his chances in the corn, then changed his mind and slid deftly underneath the vehicle. His heart sank when he punched the radio on his collar and still found only silence.

"Help me, Nika, please," Rick pleaded. "I'm sorry I put you out of the car. I'll help you get home this time, please, just help me get back on the road!"

If she shows her face, I'm gonna snap her little neck!

Nika didn't answer. Rick could only hear the sound of wind rustling through the cornfield.

"Nika? Are you still there?"

He felt her before he saw her. Her face appeared at the front of the car as she slid toward him; reaching out one tiny arm at a time and pulling herself closer until their noses touched. Rick screamed and tried to crawl backward but the belt in his pants snagged on a muffler clamp.

"What's wrong, Daddy? Don't you love me anymore?" All he could do was look deep into her eyes, deep into those inky pools of darkness, where a movie played with him as the star; standing over her lifeless body floating just beneath the surface of the soapy water.

Rick opened his mouth to scream again but Nika reached up with her arm and forced her fist into between his teeth and over his tongue, shoving the length of it down his throat. His body shook as he suffocated; she buried her arm up to the shoulder and held it there, never once letting go of her eye contact. Rick's eyes widened with amazement as the lights went out and the world went *blank*.

The computer display flickered on and the radio on his shoulder buzzed.

"RP – this is dispatch. Come in, if you're still out there. Forget that call. Apparently, it was just some kids pranking us. Go on and call it a night. Out."

Foreword

Raised by my great grandmother, I had a list of rules to learn and sing. I couldn't go into her room without permission, I couldn't sit on her bed, and, most of all, I couldn't bother her things.

When she passed and I had to sort her estate, I had this overwhelming sense of responsibility and excitement, but I also felt as if I was committing a terrible unforgiving act and she would suddenly appear in front of me and sharply remind me of her rules.

When it was all done, I had found nothing shocking or exciting, but looking through the things she had collected over nearly 100 years, really helped me understand her a little more.

I wonder what people will think when they go through my things?

Her Things

"Just tell the story, Willie, stop stalling!"

"I'm tryin' to tell y'all the story, but you keep interrupting me!" Willie yelled from across the tiny room. Normally, I'd be ready to cuff him upside his bald head but his voice cracked and I could tell he was shaking underneath his clothes, so I let it go.

"Alright, well, keep your voice down! No use hiding in here if you gonna raise your voice and give us away!" I softened my tone and tried to calm him down. I peeked through the curtain to look around outside; nothing but wind whipping the flag against the wood of the shed. A cat ran across the walkway and climbed the tree, then perched on a branch, curling its tail back and forth. I watched a few moments longer to see if something might be after it, pulling the curtain over when it seemed safe.

The door was blocked with the crates of canning jars my wife keeps in the shed for the cold weather. I hated when Viola boiled the crap out of the peaches, peppers, and apples to pour into jars – what was the point of it when you could just buy it in the store? It smelled funny, and I also hated hauling the jars to the shed when she finished.

But today, I'm thankful for those dozens and dozens of jars of slimy, disgusting fruit. Me and Phil were using the crates to sit down in the shed and listen to Willie tell his story. The other crates were being used to keep out whatever had scared Willie half to death.

We stacked them about six feet high, which was hard because Willie is the tallest of us three and he is only about five foot eight, but we stood on our tiptoes and pushed that last box up on top to give the stack some weight. It might hold her out for a while, depends on how tired she would be from the walk over here. When she was alive, she never liked to walk much. Could be why she was big as a house.

Mable and Willie's house was about a mile away but she would always get on the riding lawnmower and ride over to sit and play Spades with my wife, Viola — I call her Vi. Mable had to ride the lawnmower because she stopped fitting in the car years ago when she hit 600 pounds. So whenever she wanted to go somewhere, she would pull herself up on the lawnmower and go riding off, looking like she was searching for some grass to cut. But we all knew better.

It was a sight to see! Her rolling down the side of the dirt road at about five miles an hour, wearing a bicycle helmet in case she fell off, the mower would be mostly hidden by the folds of that big flowered mumu she wore all the time, so it looked like she had tires coming out of her ass.

Everybody got a good laugh out of that, even the school kids. My Vi was her only friend and Vi never laughed at her. She was real patient and kind to her, even though Mable was a mean old thing. Mean as a snake, she was! But Viola was nice to her and nobody else could laugh at her when my Vi was around. That's why when Mable got ran over a few weeks ago by the garbage truck, Vi was so upset that she went to stay at her mother's house in Springfield, a few miles away. She said she couldn't stand to pass by the spot where Mable got hit, she kept seeing her body tossed on the side of the road like trash waiting to be picked up. Vi said that every time she drove down the road at night, she thought she saw Mable rolling by on the lawnmower.

Anyway, Willie came rushing over about an hour ago, breathing like he was having an asthma attack and snotting all over the place. It took me a minute to understand what he was saying, but when he finally calmed down, what he said was the reason for us hiding in the shed now.

I used my cellphone to call Phil to come over and bring his shotgun, that's how Phil ended up in here with us. I guess you're thinking, why didn't I call the police instead of Phil? Well, I was gonna call the police next – I figured Phil would get there first since he could just run across the field; but after we barricaded ourselves in here, I found out that I dropped my phone whilst we were running, and nobody wanted to unblock the door so I could go back out to get it.

"Go on, Willie, tell it from the beginning again – I missed the beginning cuz you told Henry before I got here!" Phil said, cupping his hands on his knees as he sat on the wooden crate.

Willie took a deep breath and begun again.

"You know I been going crazy over there since Mable left. Seems like I could hear her voice every time I lay down to sleep. I could hear her calling for help from the side of the road," Willie removed his cap and scratched furiously at his bald head; so deeply that you could see welts rise up in the skin. I looked at the hand holding the cap, it was still shaking.

"Well that's normal, Willie, you guys were married a real long time, its normal for you to think you hear her all over the house –"

"No, no," Willie shook his head. "This ain't normal, man. I know normal, this ain't normal. I *heard* her. I wasn't sleeping, I wasn't under no medication – I *heard* her sitting in her reclining chair in the front room. The springs was squeaking like they used to do when she sat down."

I looked at Phil to back me up but he just leaned on his knees and looked at his shoes. Phil had lost his wife some years ago and he used to get all worked up in the middle of the night, thinking she was in the house with him. Took him a while to get over it. And it took him climbing up on top of the woman that worked at the pharmacy where he went to get sleeping pills. Yep, that helped him get over it too.

But this wasn't the time for me to suggest something like that to Willie. Especially not when we were hiding in the shed in fear.

"Go on, Willie," I urged him, I wanted to get to the end of the story – but then again, I didn't, because I could already hear the howling in the distance and I knew we didn't have no wolves out that way. I didn't want to hear him say it; as long as he didn't say it, it wouldn't be real. But I was holding on to Phil's shotgun just the same.

"I figured I'd make myself busy," Willie continued. "I hadn't cleaned out her stuff yet, I kept putting that off, I wasn't ready. But I figured it would help get my mind off of things, you know, if I sorted through them and gave them away to the church for somebody in need."

"You touched her things?" Phil was suddenly paying attention.

Willie nodded his head. "The truth is, I thought it would make me feel better, seeing her stuff and touching them, it might make me feel close to her again for a little while."

The one thing Mable hated was for somebody to touch her things. The whole town knew that because whenever Willie bothered something of hers, you could hear her screaming at the top of her lungs and her voice carried through the trees for what seemed like miles away. It didn't matter if they were in the house or in the field or out in town at one of the little retail shops, she would go completely insane if Willie went into her purse to get spare change or even reached across the table to take a French fry off her plate. It was *hers* and she didn't share.

It was embarrassing to witness because Willie would just cower and shake while she screamed at him, spit flying everywhere and her fists raised like she was about to beat him. I never saw her hit him, but I saw him with plenty of bruises like she was whipping him pretty good when she got the chance. He never said, and I never asked. I figured when he got tired enough of it, he knew where the shotgun shells were.

Willie took a deep breath and continued. I was trying to listen to him and listen at the same time to the howling that seemed to be getting closer. My fingers tightened on the handle of the shotgun. Whatever was out there was about to get an ass full of lead if it came messing with us tonight.

"I had to use a crowbar to bust the lock off the door to her closet. I never even knew she had a lock on it. I just never touched it so I assumed it had a regular doorknob like the other closets in the house. I can't believe she put a *lock* on it."

"That's pretty bold there, Willie," said Phil.

"Yeah, *pret-ty* bold!" Willie agreed. "I mean, that's *my* house! How you gonna put locks on the house that I built from scratch way before I even met you? And not even tell me or give me a key?"

I just shook my head. He musta forgot this was Mable we were talking about. Mable did whatever she wanted and he couldn't stop her. We all knew that.

"So what happened when you got the lock off?" I had heard this part when he burst through my front door but I wanted him to retell it for Phil's sake so he could be up to speed with us. He ran with us to the shed when we yelled, "*RUN!*" but he really didn't understand too much what was going on. I needed him to understand why Willie was shaking and why I was still guarding the door with his shotgun even though it had six heavy cases of canning jars stacked against it.

Willie's voice cracked again. "At first I just saw blankets piled on the floor, lots of blankets, like laundry. So I laughed and thought about how funny it was that she was such a stickler for a clean house but here she was hiding dirty laundry in her closet."

Willie started tapping his leg rapidly on the floor, the heel of his shoe made a hollow sound that was probably not that loud but sounded as loud as a hammer to me since we were trying to be quiet.

"Stop it, Willie," I said, and pointed with my head to his legs. He probably didn't even realize what he was doing.

"I moved the blankets and there was just...stuff, just piles and piles and piles of...stuff."

"What kind of stuff?" Phil asked him, leaning forward as if the story had just gotten really juicy to him.

Just wait, Phil, it gets better.

"I thought they were popsicle sticks at first, just a lot of popsicle sticks, that's what I thought. You know, Mable liked her snacks a lot, and sometimes she would hide what she was eating so I wouldn't ask for none. Then when I picked up a handful, I could tell they were...bones," Willie covered his face with his hands.

"Bones? What kind of bones? Chicken bones?" Phil's eyes were wide and round, he was all ears now.

Willie shook his head, still covering his face.

"I don't know what kind of bones, but I'll tell you this – they weren't chicken."

"Tell him what you think they were, Willie. He has a right to know the whole thing. He's in this with us too, now," I urged him on. The man had a right to know. After all, he ran over when I called him and brought his gun just like I asked. Now he was in here with us and whatever was going to happen was going to happen to him too, so he oughta know what he was going to war with.

Willie took his hands away from his face.

"I think they were human bones," He said, looking Phil directly in his eyes.

Phil scoffed. "Human bones? Mannnnnn, you musta been drinking, Willie."

"Phil, I haven't had a drink since Mable died. I stopped drinking because the man that killed her was drunk and I keep thinking that he might have hit some of the school kids walking along the road going to school. I keep thinking that could have been me behind the wheel. So I won't drink anymore, in memory of Mable."

"So where would the bones come from, Willie?"

Willie hesitated.

"Go 'head, Willie. Tell him like you told me," I threw my voice into the silence.

"Phil, you remember those missing kids?"

Phil paused, then laughed, "Mannnn, you fools got me up in here with this craziness! I bet you both been drinking! What are you trying to tell me now? Mable kidnapped those kids?"

Phil stood and reached up to the crate highest on the stack.

"Let me out of here, I got a date tonight, I don't have time for this foolishness. I thought something serious was going on!" He looked at me to help him as he stretched to reached the crate.

That's when we heard the cat scream as something got after it outside of the window. I was too scared to move and didn't want to look out the curtain again, but that cat was in some kind of fight out there. It screeched and hissed for what seemed like hours but it was just a few minutes until it got silent.

We three stood and stared at each other in the shed, afraid to move or we might end up like the cat.

"What was that?" Phil whispered.

"I don't know," I answered as honestly as I could, because I didn't exactly *know*. Not yet.

"I know," Willie said and turned to Phil again. "I didn't finish telling you, but there were kid's clothes in the closet, the same clothes they said the kids were wearing when they went missing."

That was all I had needed to hear when Willie got me to run earlier. I remembered those kids, the news crew walking up and down the road talking to folks about them; the search parties walking through the woods wearing orange vests, calling their names and waving floodlights in the night. So when Willie described the clothes he found in Mable's closet, that's all I needed to hear to believe.

"There's more though," Willie whispered.

"What?" Phil's voice was cracking now.

"There was more than just those three kids. There was a pile of shoes in the back of the closet up against the wall, looked like it belonged to a bus load of kids."

I froze at this new part of the story. *A bus load of kids.*

"You mean...?" Phil sat back down on the crate. "The bus?"

Willie nodded. "*The* bus."

Years ago, back when Mable was still small enough to fit through her front door without turning sideways, a small church bus full of middle-schoolers from vacation bible school ran off the road on the way back from an outing. The bus was found head first in the ravine some yards off the main road; whatever the rocks hadn't destroyed, the rushing river had finished. The driver's mangled body had smashed through the front window and hung over the hood as if he had made some effort to escape but death caught him just before he met freedom.

The children's bodies...well, the children were never found. Not a single one. It was assumed that the river had carried them away so fast that they merged into the big divide where the water turned into an angry roaring lake full of dangerous man-eating sharks.

No one had ever *seen* any sharks but there had to be sharks. As big as that lake was, there had to be shark and jellyfish and all kinds of hungry things. Dogs disappeared from the area and their carcasses would wash up on the edge days later, so there just had to be something in there!

Searches came up empty and eventually people gave up and accepted that the kids were gone. Even though it didn't make any sense, the truth was even more frightening.

Phil finally spoke. "Okay, if all of this is true –"

"It is true." Willie interrupted him. "I got no reason to lie!"

"Okay, I'm just saying – if you say all of this is there and you saw the evidence and everything, what difference does it make now? I say you bury all of that stuff and let it go! What are you thinking? You wanna call the police and have them crawling around your house and digging up all of those memories? You want your house to be known as the house of horrors?"

Phil stood up and got close to Willie's face as he finished his take on it all.

"Mable's gone now! So if she knew something about those kids, she took it with her to her grave!"

"That's just it, Phil," Willie said softly. "She's not gone."

Now *this* is another part I heard as I was running across the yard with Willie at my heels. Phil was a little further behind, running in his long underwear and his eating shirt – he called it an eating shirt because it was big and roomy and ugly as hell! He wore it whenever he barbecued and made a mess of himself eating the ribs. He didn't care much about getting all of the stains out of it because it had so many colors and patterns in it that you wouldn't even see the stains.

He was running behind me and Willie in his eating shirt, waving his rifle in the air, yelling, "I'm coming, I got my gun, who I gotta shoot?"

And I heard Willie panting next to me, "She's back! Mable's back!"

Now this wouldn't have come as so much of a shock to me if I hadn't already been trying to process the dead kids in the closet – or, I should say, the *remains* of the dead kids in the closet. I would have just patted Willie on the shoulder and guided him back to his house, checked through the house to show him that there was no ghosts, and then I would have gone on home to climb in bed with my Vi.

But the howling in the woods started after he got to my house, and like I said, we don't have no wolves up here.

Willie and Phil looked at me when the scratching started on the wall of the shed. I don't know why they're looking at me, I don't have the answers. I'm not even the tallest! I was kinda hoping Phil would save us, that's why I called him: he brought the shotgun but I really thought he would have brought an extra gun or two tucked in his waistband to give me and Willie. He always talked about his days being in a gang back when he was young and had processed hair. Why the hell does he only have one shotgun now?

I'm thinking now that that was a waste of my minutes, calling him when I needed help. I shoulda called the police. Or my Vi.

Scratch. Scratch. Scrape.

This shed is only made out of wood. I wanted to use brick but them damn bricks cost too much and Vi wouldn't go for it. I bet she'll wish she had listened to me when she gets home tomorrow, the joke is on her! I almost laughed at the thought of her looking at what used to be our shed and having to admit that I was right about the brick.

The men started huddling in closer to me. I thought about just shooting through the wall but if I missed, then, well, there's a hole for her to get in.

I started thinking again about my Vi. I was enjoying the peace and solitude of her being gone to her mom's. She was a nag and a half but she was *my* nag and a half. I liked sleeping in late, walking around the house in my raggedy drawers, belching and scratching my nuts without her squealing at me to stop. But right about now, I was wishing she was home. Not only did I miss cuddling up under her big ass at night, but I was hoping she would come home and notice me missing and come looking for me. Maybe find us in the shed and I could yell at her through the window to call the police, then get in the car and drive like hell as far away as she could.

Mable might be nice to her since that was her only friend. But then again, that was the old Mable. The new Mable is probably really pissed off that Willie messed with her things.

Foreword

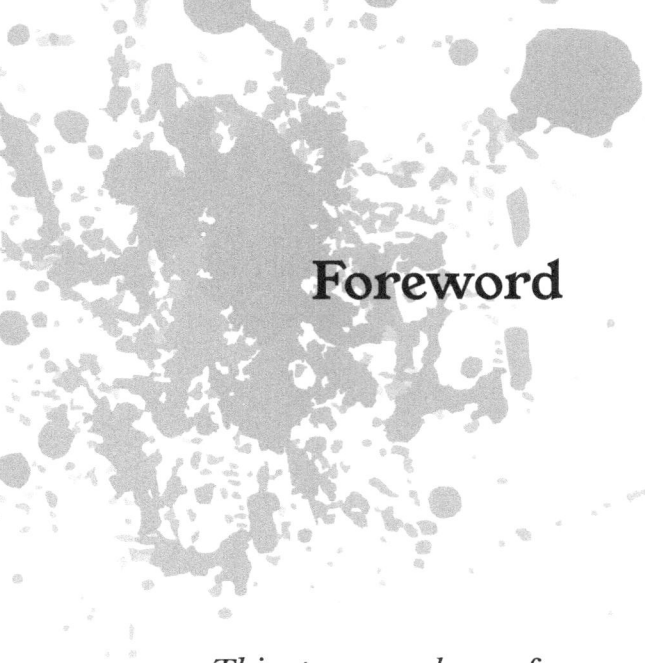

This story was borne from some of my grandmother's words of wisdom.

As my sister and I became young women, she would always tell us to be careful with whom we shared our bodies, because we were allowing a bit of that person's soul to bind with ours, therefore, they would always be with us. I never really 'got it' until I was well into adulthood, navigating my way through a relationship minefield.

But her words make me wonder... what happens if you share your soul with someone that you hate?

Baby Mine

THEY WERE ALL SO weak. So useless. Stray puppies, they were. Throw them a scrap of meat and they never leave your doorstep; they just hang around the door, pissing in the flowers.

He was still sitting on the edge of the bed, watching her brush her hair in the mirror as he slowly pulled on his socks. His eyes were watering; she knew because she caught a glimpse of the tears just before she turned her back on him. Jessica imagined he was holding his head up in some gallant effort to keep the tears from spilling over. He was a crier. She discovered that early on in the relationship. He cried over every damn thing. Not full *boo-hoo-hoo* crying but his eyes would fill with tears and he'd have to dab at them with tissue.

So fucking pitiful, she thought to herself, as she rubbed her temples furiously with her fingertips. *I just wish he would leave – crawl out on the sidewalk and die in the heat like an earthworm – just leave!*

Her head was beginning to hurt and his scent was pervading the air, filling her nose and her lungs; he smelled like meat, raw meat. She wanted to gag. She didn't notice it the night before, but she could smell it now. She wanted to gag. When did that start - that smell? She didn't notice the night before, but she could smell it now. Waves of nausea blurred her vision and she fought the urge to run to the bathroom and throw up.

Jessica tried to avoid the pathetic sight of him in the vanity mirror but her eyes wandered to him again. *Why doesn't he just leave?*

"Your coat is in the hall closet," she spoke finally, hoping to spur some acceleration in his movement.

He stood then, naked and unremarkable, turning his head in a 180 degree angle as he looked around the bedroom. Suddenly, he bent and reached under the bed, emerging with his underwear clutched in his hand. He bent and pulled them slowly up one leg first then the other, moving as if his body were riddled with arthritis.

Tighty-whities - for real? Jessica shook her head when he stood up straight and she saw what he had pulled onto his body. *Remind me again just HOW you got back in my bed?* The sight of him standing there in those snug white briefs just irritated her all over again, because she was clearly off her game if she didn't spot them when they stumbled into her bedroom and removed their clothing. Oh yes, that's right, the margaritas. They always blurred her vision and softened her resolve, especially after the third or fourth.

Steve tried to start a conversation but she refused to face him, keeping her shoulders hunched over and staring at a spot of red nail polish in the carpet. He stood on the other side of the room and apologized again, then mumbled goodbye as he exited the bedroom.

"You're not even going to walk me out, huh?" He asked, pausing briefly in the doorway.

"You know the way," replied Jessica over her shoulder without meeting his eyes.

What did I ever see in him? She asked herself, staring at him in disbelief.

Their breakup had been so hurtful that Jessica had retired from dating for a while. Not intending for it to be permanent, but she needed a break after such a long and dysfunctional relationship. She needed to reclaim her power and get to know herself again. She was certain of what she did not want in her next relationship - anything that remotely resembled Steve; the only thing she wanted her new prospective partner to have in common with Steve was that they both breathed oxygen. She wanted to stay as far away from anything that looked or sounded like that man - his name couldn't even start with the letter "S".

In fact, she had grown to hate Steve so much that she considered even eliminated men with ANY of the same letters in their name, first and last. It was *that* kind of hate. The kind that kept her up at night for the first few weeks after their breakup. She would lie awake wondering if he had any remorse for the damage he had done; then she would imagine all sorts of horrible things happening to him, from car accidents to skin-ravaging diseases. Every fantasy ended with his funeral. She even fantasized about *attending* his funeral. That seemed to be the only thing that gave her comfort, imagining him lying in a casket, stiff and cold, and her walking up the casket and smiling. That vision gave her a perfect kind of peace that allowed her to finally find sleep.

But....he had looked so...delicious...when they met at the restaurant last night. He dressed so nicely for their date and smelled like you wanted to melt in his arms and let him put you in the trunk of his car – as long as he held you close while you carried your limp body to the parking lot. Just *that* good. She sat at the table staring into his eyes and almost forgot what a bastard he really was or how much of an asshole he had been to her when they broke up six months prior. Staring into his mouth while he talked, she watched his tongue slide around the Cajun-peppered shrimp and she quivered slightly, remembering how good that same tongue used to feel on her body. Never mind that he had a disgusting habit of eating with his mouth open so one could see every step of the beginning digestion, she had decided by dessert that she was going to sleep with him again that night. As much for old time's sake as it was, simply, because her body was calling for it.

Never mind that he was a despicable loser or that he had a girlfriend waiting for him at home - yes, she was well aware that he had a girlfriend, despite his insistence that he'd broken up with the girl he last cheated on her with. He kept one eye locked on his phone, and sent calls straight to voicemail with a swipe of his finger - the standard profile of a taken man out on a date. She was more than familiar with that behavior. He'd sent many of her calls to voicemail when she was the one sitting at home waiting.

Jessica took no pleasure in playing the role of "that whore you were out with" tonight, but she had needs, and Steve just got lucky, so to speak, when he called her phone on an evening when she was feeling lonely, and, well, sexually frustrated.

She was tired of the dating scene, fresh off of another first date with a creep she'd met online - and horny -

mostly horny. She saw Steve's name pop up on her cell phone screen and instead of flashing back to how he stole her debit card and withdrew two thousand from her bank account and lying about it - she remembered how he made her legs quake when he used to spend hours between them, exploring and teasing and making her dizzy and weak.

"I can't believe you're going out with that fuckin' loser," Angel scoffed as she watched Jessica dress for her date. "I told you, if it's that tight, my coworker Tony has been trying to hook up with you for years, all you gotta do is call him."

Jessica twisted and turned in the mirror, trying to decide on an outfit for the date.

"Why don't I have an ass?" She asked Angel. "All the other black girls got asses, why don't I?" She arched her back and tried to create the illusion of a bigger bump in her lower back.

"You're too skinny," Angel replied. "Get some meat on ya bones, the ass will come. Stop eating like a white girl."

Jessica frowned at her failure to create a shapely rear. "I don't eat like a white girl, I like to eat healthy, you should try it."

"See, that's that white girl conditioning you got from going to private school. If you had gone to Central like everybody else - you'd have an ass," Angel concluded and waved her hand as if the determination was final.

"Okay, that makes a lot of sense," Jessica replied, rolling her eyes. "I can always count on you for hood logic."

"That's right, you sure can! You still didn't answer me though - want me to hook you up with Tony? I can call him for you. If you just want a booty call, he got you too, I'm sure he won't have a problem helping you out."

"Does Tony know that you try to pimp him out? Because I swear I heard you offer him to Cresha the other day when we were at lunch."

Angel laughed. "I was just messing with Cresha, trying to cheer her up. But for real, he's always asking me about you, and he just separated from his wife so it's like they say - everything happens for a reason."

"What's the reason?" Jessica returned to the closet and picked out a long white maxi dress with a low dip in the cleavage.

"You know - Tony is free and single now and you're about to make the biggest mistake of your life, so he can come over and help redirect your feelings away from Steve the loser. By the way, the dress is perfect."

"I know! I love this!" Jessica smoothed the fabric across her body and beamed at herself in the mirror, pleased with the contrast of the white against her skin the color of creamy hazelnut butter.

"You planning to go screw, ain't you?" Angel peered at her cousin through disapproving eyes. "Ain't that asshole did enough wrong to you to last a lifetime?"

"Who said I was planning to screw? I just want him to see what he's missing," replied Jessica.

"He already knows what he's missing, Jess - your purse, your car, your good credit, let's see, what else? Oh yeah, your head game, he's missing that too. You don't need to go and show him nothing, he already knows, that's why he called you."

"Well, I want to rub it in his face. I really want him to see me and know that he can't touch me. I want him to see how happy I am without him and then just walk away."

"You know how you show somebody that you're happy without them? You don't give them any of your time. You keep not answering when they call and you ignore them," Angel said, shaking her head in disgust. "This-" she pointed a finger of disapproval at Jessica's dress. "-this is what you do when you still got feelings for a nigga."

Jessica slid her silver bangles across her wrist and added a couple of dramatic shakes for emphasis. She wasn't listening to her cousin. Now was not the time. Angel had a solid relationship with a fiancée who owned two successful restaurants - what did she know? What did she understand about lonely nights and cold spots in the bed where no one seemed to ever lie? She wanted what Angel had, and thus far that had eluded her. She had everything else, education, career, financial security, but true love continued to escape her grasp. Everything else came relatively easy but love was the one thing she had to work for and she was at the point in her life where she decided she was tired of waiting. Steve's surprise phone call had caught her completely off guard and she wasn't sure whether it was a sign to forgive and forget, or a reminder of the life from which she had escaped and motivation to keep moving forward.

She and Steve had shared a passionate yet turbulent history, ending in an ugly and tearful fight over yet another of his messy indiscretions. Steve was a serial cheater and pathological liar, but he was also a quick-witted, smooth-talking Lothario of the highest order. Their five-year relationship was fraught with trouble from the first date, when Jessica was confronted in a restaurant bathroom by one of Steve's former girlfriends, who proceeded to rattle off a list of Steve's faults and habits in rapid-fire precision. Jessica shrugged her off as being a casebook "bitter ex" and went on to create her own experiences with Steve - that eventually began to distinctly mirror those of that first "bitter ex".

Years went by and the bodies piled up; that bathroom encounter was just one of many ambushes Jessica endured, where women made it their mission to inform her of who and what Steve really was - but she didn't listen. She frequently changed her cellphone number to avoid the *"bitter bitch brigade"* as Steve liked to call them. She moved comfortably into her new digs in the city of Denial, and went about redecorating the place with fresh paint and new furniture to make it a home for her and Steve.

Even when the birth announcement showed up in her mailbox, Steve had a story for that - it wasn't his. How could it be? He'd only worked with that crazy girl for a year and he barely spoke to her, but somehow she was obsessed with him and was telling everybody that he was her baby's daddy. *Don't you trust me?* He would declare with those soft brown puppy dog eyes. And in short time, he would have Jessica undressed and screaming in the throes of passion; the birth announcement tossed in the bedroom trash and completely forgotten.

Surely, he couldn't be lying about a baby, could he? She would ask herself. *Who does that?* He'd have to be some kind of sociopath to have a child by a woman he worked with, yet deny it and carry on his relationship with his oblivious girlfriend with whom he shared an apartment, with whom he shared a *life*. Again, who does that?

A week after the birth announcement, Jessica left some important papers at home and had to return during lunch to retrieve them. She was shocked to find Steve's car in the driveway when he should have been at work himself; he usually left earlier than she did and

Jessica had kissed him goodbye that very morning.

She found him under the covers, fast asleep and snoring so loudly that he didn't hear her enter the apartment or call his name. She stood by the bedside watching him sleep and felt uneasiness in the pit of her stomach. That same uneasiness she was used to feeling every time something didn't quite sound right until he appeared to smooth it over with his smile and his perfectly reasonable explanations, and of course a little bit of his magic penis thrown in for good measure. She picked up the folder she needed from the bedside table and tip-toed lightly out of the room without waking him. When she got back in her car, she pulled out her cellphone and dialed the number to Steve's office at which point she was greeted by the cheerful voice of Angie, the company secretary.

"Good morning, can I speak to Steve, please?"

Uncomfortable pause.

"I'm sorry, but….Steve is no longer employed here. Is there someone else I can get to assist you?" replied Angie.

Jessica's heart sank with what seemed like an audible thud that reverberated off the windows of the car. Tears welled in her eyes as she struggled to compose herself and finish the call.

"I'm sorry; did you say that he no longer works there?"

"Yes?" Angie confirmed her statement.

"Um, can you tell me when he *stopped* working there?"

"I don't think I can give out any more information….wait," Angie suddenly whispered into the phone. "Is this Jessica? His girlfriend?" She and Jessica had met briefly several times over the past year at various company functions. Since she was responsible for fielding the sales calls to the agents, she would certainly be familiar with Jessica's voice.

Jessica replied weakly, her heart beating loudly in her chest, "Yes, it's Jessica."

There was that uncomfortable pause again.

More hesitation and a few moments of dead silence. You could almost detect through the phone the sound of the secretary carefully choosing her words, trying to decide between the rules written in the company handbook and the unwritten rules of sistahood.

"Jessica, Steve got fired two weeks ago - he didn't tell you?" Angie whispered sharply into the receiver. "Don't you two still live together?"

Jessica froze. Steve had been leaving for work every day as if he still had a job, and then apparently circling back and returning to bed.

"No, I didn't know," Jessica replied weakly, her voice cracking.

More silence as Angie weighed her choices and then decided to go full girl code.

"Did you know about the baby? He got fired because of the baby! I can't say anymore and please don't say I told you this much or I'll lose my job! But girl, be careful, okay?" Angie hung up the phone without waiting for a response.

Jessica sat in her car with her eyes filling with tears and absorbed the information she had just been given. The secretary had jeopardized her job in order to help her and Jessica was feeling grateful to Angie but angry that she had been so stupid for so long. She wanted to call back and ask for the contact information of the woman who'd had the baby, but she knew she shouldn't push her luck, so instead she navigated to the internet on her phone and searched for the website of the hospital whose name appeared on the birth announcement. Before Steve had taken the birth announcement out of her hands and started peeling off her clothes, she managed to quickly read and commit to memory some of the details, like the date of birth and the baby's name. The baby boy was named after Steve, making it even easier to locate the birth announcement at the hospital's online nursery.

Her hands shook as she stared at her phone. It was there clear as day.

Baby Boy Steve Anderson Hawking Jr. He was two weeks old on the day that Jessica confirmed his birth and called her two brothers to come over and help her move Steve out of her apartment. She sat in the driveway and waited; her brothers showed up together within 15 minutes of her distress call, entering her apartment and proceeding to kick Steve's ass until Jessica tearfully begged them to stop. Steve left bloody and bruised, carrying whatever he could fit into two banker's boxes, and that was the last time they spoke.

Until he called two nights ago.

Her stomach was bubbling now; what had she eaten that was causing this kind of a reaction? Seafood. It had to be the seafood. She wondered if the shrimp cocktail she'd consumed at their dinner was somehow responsible for the queasiness she was now feeling.

She listened for the sound of Steve closing the front door on his way out, and the roar of his car engine parked in the front. When she was sure he was gone, she felt the first tidal wave rush from the pits of her stomach and she just barely made it to the floor in front of the toilet to empty her gut into the bowl. It came up so fast and forceful that she didn't have time to hold back her hair, and her braids dangled alongside her face and dipped into the foul water as she hovered. The sight of her hair being splattered with bits of digested food and stomach acid caused her to become even more nauseated and she continued hurling until her stomach could produce no more. After a few dry heaves, she reached up with a weak hand and pulled the flush lever, then passed out on the floor with wet smelly braids scattered across her face.

The sharp smell of burnt coffee cut through her nostrils, forcing her to open her eyes. The coffee maker had turned itself on as programmed but the decanter was scorching. Jessica stirred on the bathroom floor and foggily assessed her predicament from the cold tile. She rubbed her eyes and smelled the sour odor of vomit and unwashed fingers, then winced as her eyes began to burn. Pushing herself up by her elbows, her mind began to replay the earlier events; she had passed out after the violent retching episode and thumped her head a nicely on the way to meet with the floor. She reached up and rubbed the back of her head and felt a tender spot, then felt the dampness of her braids lying against her clothing.

"Oh my god, what is wrong with me? This shit is gross!" She felt ashamed at being in such disarray; it felt like she had emerged from a time warp and was back in her college dorm, awakening after a drunken binge with her roommates. She was far too old for this shit and her body certainly didn't recover as quickly from the strain of vomiting and the bruises from falling.

She looked at the clock on the shower wall and realized that she had lost a large block of time. That scared her, along with the realization that coffee was indeed burning and soon the smoke detectors would sound off if she didn't get her ass up from the floor.

Ignoring the pain, she used the sink to pull herself up and push off into the hallway and down the stairs, immediately losing her balance as the dizziness swept across her brain. She reached for the stair rail and caught the metal bannister holder between her fingers, yelling out in pain as her fingers twisted and snapped and failed to grab hold. Her body slid the remainder of the way down the stairs, landing with a hard thump at the bottom.

As if on cue, the smoke alarm beeped twice and then a siren pierced the air. Every nerve in Jessica's body was alive and fighting for attention. She wanted to cry, scream, curl up in the fetal position, hold her breath, and throw up again, but she needed to will herself to roll over and crawl to the kitchen counter just a few yards away. She made it, slowly and painfully, and grasped the cabinet knob to pull her body up from the floor. The pot cracked loudly from the heat just as she managed to focus her eyes and take in the situation. The fresh coffee dried and then scorched, turning into a potential disaster that could have burned down her apartment.

After securing the danger and fanning the smoke detector back into silence, Jessica stood leaning against the counter, holding her stomach and trying to quell the sickness rising to her throat. Surely there couldn't be anything left in her stomach to dispense! She spun around to the sink just in time to hit the handle and start the water flowing to rinse away the bile erupting from her stomach.

Regaining her balance, she managed to stand upright before the room began spinning and her vision blurred. She leaned across the sink to crank open the window for fresh air, however, the movement caused her lower back to ache as if she was being poked with needles.

I think it's time to get to Urgent Care, she spoke out loud. She knew it was highly unlikely that she was in any condition to drive, nevertheless, she held onto the sink for a few minutes to steady herself, then took slow deliberate steps across the room toward her purse. Luckily, her cell phone was still inside. She and Steve had been so caught up in their fiery lust the night before that she hadn't given her phone a second thought as they came through the front door practically melding into each other's bodies, lips meeting lips, tongue swiping tongue, hands exploring what used to be familiar territory but now seemed like a newly discovered body of land.

She had tossed her bag on the counter, giving herself to the moment, and for the first time in months, allowed her cell phone to be more than a few feet away from her hand for an extended period of time. In this case, that turned out to be a blessing because she would never have made it back up the stairs to retrieve the phone and locate Steve's number in her Recent Calls. She pressed the phone icon to automatically dial his number and prayed silently that he would pick up quickly. He didn't. The voicemail answered.

"This subscriber's mailbox is full. Please try your call again later."

Jessica winced as she realized that his box was likely full due to his current girlfriend searching frantically for him last night while he was pounding away inside of her body and whispering lies into her ear. She didn't feel the least bit guilty about it when it was happening and her stomach quivered briefly as she pictured him gripping her braids from behind as he moaned and poured himself into her. But now that she needed him, the guilt swept over her and brought tears to her eyes. She had been in that spot before herself, sitting at home dialing and redialing his number, leaving long angry and tearful voicemails while he stretched out in someone else's bed.

Why was she calling him anyway? She had just tossed him out earlier and declared him a lost cause. She pushed the button to speak the name of her cousin Angel and auto-dial her number.

Angel's phone clicked over to voicemail without even ringing, so she redialed Steve and prayed silently for him to pick up. To hear his voice at this moment would bring her peace; she desperately needed his help and as she listened to the unanswered rings, she told herself that she would say and promise him anything to get him to return and take her to the hospital.

After three more redials, Steve finally answered and then just held the phone without speaking.

"Hello?" She felt a twinge of sudden joy as she gripped the phone tightly to her ear. She needed to hear his voice!

"Yes?" The voice was cold and emotionless.

"Steve?"

"Yes?"

"I need help!" Jessica couldn't hold back the tears as they burst forth at last. She shook and cried loudly into the phone.

"I'm sick, Steve, I need to go to the hospital!"

Silence.

"What do you mean sick?" He asked finally.

"I mean, I'm really sick! I think I got food poisoning last night at the restaurant, I don't know, but I've been throwing up since you left and I passed out and I feel like I'm gonna DIE!" Jessica cried, emphasizing the last word. Her words tumbled out in a rush and she massaged each one with a coat of tears.

"Please help me, Steve! I think something is really wrong and I'm scared to stay here! I can't drive myself or I would!"

She could hear someone speak in the background and Steve took the phone away from his ear and spoke off in the distance. "I'll be right there, its work, babe!"

Her heart dropped. He was at home. With her. And she was his babe. That phrase told her everything she needed to know. He wouldn't be coming to take her to any hospital because he was with his *babe* and she was last night's entertainment.

Suddenly she felt angry. "Look, I just need a ride to the hospital, that's all. I am really sick! If you can get me there, I can get Angel to take it from there. Please?"

"Can't you get her to take you? I'm kinda busy right now."

"I tried, Steve, I can't get her on the phone." She managed to stop the tears from falling down her cheeks but couldn't stop them from choking her words. "Can you just do this for me?" She swallowed hard and added, "I need you."

His voice mocked her. "You need me? That's a new one. You just kicked me out this morning. You sure seemed fine then. When did this sickness start? Because you were fine when you were telling me to get the hell out." He finished his mini-rant with a sneeze.

"Steve, I know you're mad and you have every right to be but I'm telling you that I'm really sick right now and if I had anyone else to call then I would. I just need your help. Please!"

The woman on Steve's end had now moved closer to him because Jessica clearly heard her say, "Get off the phone, baby, we gotta get ready for tonight!"

She heard what sounded like a shared kiss and that gave her the answer, he would not be coming to drive her to any hospital. He was home and he couldn't care less about her, just as she couldn't care less about him that morning when she wanted him gone.

She didn't torture herself by waiting for another response, she clicked the button to end the call and dialed 911 for an ambulance.

Jessica waited on the sofa for the paramedics. Sitting still and trying not to move because every movement of her limbs made her feel as if she would pass out. She willed herself to stay awake until she heard the sirens getting closer. She strained her neck to see if the doorknob was unlocked - of course it was. Far be it for Steve to care enough about her to make sure he locked the door on his way out. But it was a good thing that it was unlocked because she didn't think she would be able to rise and let the paramedics in.

The ambulance squealed to a halt in front of her apartment door and within minutes Jessica was flanked by three fast-moving and fast talking medical technicians fussing over her, shining a light in her eyes, taking her pulse and asking her questions, while she leaned against the back of the sofa and tried to keep from blacking out

"Miss, Miss, stay with us now, can you talk? Do you think you can stand? Is there anyone else here with you?"

Jessica shook her hand to indicate a no to all of his questions and just as she fell asleep, she felt her body being lifted from the cushions and stretched out on a firm clean-smelling mattress. She closed her eyes and dreamed of Steve.

"You didn't have to go through all of this to get me to come see you, girl," Angel was leaning over the hospital bed, peering into Jessica's face. "All you had to do was call!" She joked but her eyes showed a mixture of worry and fear.

Jessica tried to separate her eyelids but her lashes had fused together from the tears and old mascara. Her mouth was dry and her throat raw and sore. She raised her arms and forced her crusted lashes apart to look at the IV line dispensing a clear fluid into her veins, and then she turned back toward the sound of Angel's voice over her face.

"Are you going to wake up now and stop playing?" Angel asked, her cracking voice betraying her attempt to lighten the mood with humor.

"Jessica? Say something to me before I slap you!"

Jessica managed a weak smile and Angel pounced.

"See! I knew you were foolin'! Making me go through all of this trouble! Why didn't you just tell me you had a bun in the oven and you just wanted some of that pregnant sex from Steve?"

Wait, what did she say?

"Here I was worried about you, thinking you was about to get back involved with that fool and you was just trying to scratch that pregnant itch. I heard about y'all pregnant women - but I thought you got horny toward the middle and end of it, not right at the beginning!" Angel continued. "And then you don't even tell me who you been fucking with! Who's the daddy?"

Jessica forced herself to speak. "What are you talking about?" She whispered, wincing over the pain in her throat.

Angel laughed. "Oh, so we're gonna play dumb now? Okay, cuz. I thought we were BFFs? You didn't even tell me that you were dating anybody, much less getting some! No wonder you were sick, you still running around here wearing tight clothes AND you been drinking - you know you're not supposed to do that! Unless you trying to get rid of this baby, and that can't be it because from the looks of things, you waited too long to do that!"

Jessica shook her head angrily. "No! No! I don't know what you're talking about!"

"You didn't know for real?" Angel stopped joking and stroked her arm that held the IV tubing taped to the inside of the elbow.

Jessica shook her head again. She was in shock. How could she be pregnant when she had not had sex in six months before last night? And if she had gotten pregnant last night - surely she wouldn't be having symptoms barely less than 24 hours later?

Besides all of that - she *could not* be pregnant because she was unable to conceive due to a botched abortion when she was only 17 years old. She cringed as she remembered that dark time in her young life. After months of sneaky sweaty clandestine sex with her secret boyfriend - the 26 year old married church choir director - she suddenly missed two consecutive periods and had to throw up inside the school bathroom a handful of times directly after cheerleading practice. She wrote off the queasiness to all of the bouncing, jostling, splits and flips of the intense athletic session, but she couldn't deny the missed periods, and when Angel stole a pregnancy test from the local drugstore, they met in her bathroom to confirm that which needed no further confirmation.

She was 17 and pregnant and there was no way she could have this baby. If word got out that she was pregnant, her mother would be so ashamed of what the church would think, she would probably move them out of town and change their names. That's after she beat the hell *and* the baby out of Jessica. And she definitely couldn't let it be known that she was pregnant by a married man who stood in front of the church every Sunday and lead the choir in song, while his beautiful wife and child sat in the audience staring at him adoringly. The church could never find out that Jessica had been meeting him in the back of the church after rehearsal and allowing him to bend her over the desk in his tiny office. Or, that she had pleasured him way too many times to count by leaning over the front seat of his Honda and filling her mouth with every inch of him.

Only Angel knew. And God. But Angel was going to help her find a way out. That way out came in the form of a hastily scribbled phone number on a post-it note stuck to the inside of her locker. Sheila Boom Boom was her name; fixing unwanted pregnancies on the cheap was her game. She had "fixed it" for a few of the other cheerleaders who found themselves in that same predicament.

The hour that Jessica spent writhing in pain on a blood-stained sheet draped across a kitchen table almost cost her life. She ended up in the hospital the next day with septic shock and the doctor gazed pitifully upon her face and held her hand as she gently explained that her cervix was ruptured and torn by the crudely performed abortion and she would never be able to carry a fertilized egg. She mourned but a short time over this revelation before deciding that it was actually a blessing because she really did not want children anyway. Who wants to bring more kids into this fucked up world? She never saw that as fair, to have a child and then kick it out of the nest and tell it that life is tough, deal with it. It was actually okay with her if she never had kids.

So while she knew that she couldn't get pregnant, she still used protection to safeguard against something worse than pregnancy - disease and death. But that night with Steve, she admittedly let her urges get the best of her and she failed to reach into her nightstand and pull out the condoms. Mainly because she didn't have any. It had been a while since she'd been in a sexual relationship and she certainly didn't plan on being in one this quickly. She wanted to ask him to get a condom, she knew he would have one; he always did since he was such a male whore. But it felt so good to be touched and caressed again that she didn't want to ruin the moment with technicalities and she just wanted to feel him inside of her with no filter, no barrier. She wanted to connect with him in a most intimate and completely fulfilling manner. In her head, she screamed, *make him pull out, make him pull it out!* But when she felt him tremble and jerk and she knew the moment was near, all she wanted was to feel *it*. And so she did.

And here she was.

Yet, it was impossible that she could be pregnant from *that*. But there had been no other in over six months. Surely the tests were incorrect and the doctor was getting a false reading!

Jessica tapped Angel's hand and pointed at her mouth. "Water, please?" She spoke softly, her throat searing with pain.

"Oh, okay, I don't think you can have water but I'll get you some ice chips. Your throat must hurt from the tube they stuck down there," replied Angel as she patted Jessica's arm again and left the room. "Be right back. I'll get the doctor too, now that you're awake."

The doctor entered Jessica's room about ten minutes, followed by a nervous looking Angel. Dr. Pham was a tiny Asian woman with soft concerned eyes. She approached the bedside almost hesitantly and began swiping through her tablet as she reviewed the medical information.

"Miss Jessica! How are you Miss Jessica? How you feeling?" She asked, still swiping and looking quickly from Jessica's face to the tablet screen. She stuck out her hand and felt Jessica's forehead then moved her fingers down and pressed into the sides of her neck to feel for swollen lymph nodes.

"You feel better?" She asked and whipped out a tiny light to look into Jessica's eyes before she could respond.

"Yes. but what is this my cousin was telling me about being pregnant? I can't be pregnant?"

Dr. Pham paused and looked at her, confused. "Well, you say you can't, but you are!" She began tapping into her tablet, documenting the results of her once-over. She jerked back the sheet and used one hand to feel Jessica's ankles.

"Hold this, please!" The tiny dark-haired doctor jabbed the tablet toward Angel who stood right next to her. Angel grinned and took it from her.

"Can I check my Facebook on here, doc?" She asked and giggled.

Dr. Pham smiled. 'Yes, you check your Facebook and then you post your cousin medical history all over social media! You don't want that do you?" She replied, laughing.

She turned back to Jessica. "Tell me, do this hurt?" She began poking around Jessica's belly and pressing on her abdomen and Jessica indeed felt pain in every spot the doctor applied pressure.

Dr. Pham paid close attention to her swollen belly, which had risen to form a small round curve beneath her belly button, something that Jessica had not noticed before.

"Oh yeah, you pregnant!" Dr. Pham declared with a tone of finality. "The test show you pregnant and your belly show you pregnant! You showing! You did not know?"

"Oh my God, Jessica! You're showing! How did I not see that when you had on that gorgeous white dress?" exclaimed Angel.

Dr. Pham reached for Jessica's hand and pulled it around to place on the rising mound of her growing child. Jessica drew back in horror at the feeling of her firm extended abdomen, then she placed her hand there again out of fascination, and she traced the roundness with the tips of her fingers.

She looked at Dr. Pham with wide-eyed bewilderment. "I don't understand? I can't be pregnant!"

"You been having sex?" asked Dr. Pham.

Jessica stammered. "Well, I-I-I don't know!"

"You have sex? You don't use birth control? When you have sex?"

"Well, it's been a while, I don't know!" Jessica was reluctant to reveal the events of the night before, for fear the conversation would then to questions which she could not answer about the *baby's father.*

"But, I did fall down the stairs before I called the ambulance," she tried to explain.

"You fell down the stairs?" exclaimed Angel.

Jessica nodded and swallowed more ice chips. "That's why I couldn't drive, I was too sick and weak and sore from the fall. Maybe that's from falling?" Jessica pointed at her swollen belly.

"No, no, no, that's not from falling, that's from having sex! You know where babies come from, Miss Jessica?" Dr. Pham asked and she and Angel erupted into laughter. "You have sex, you get pregnant. You pregnant, Miss Jessica. That's all there is to it. The test say you pregnant. I say you pregnant."

Dr. Pham took her tablet out of Angel's hands and resumed tapping on the screen.

"Look like you around eight to ten week. You have OB/GYN you go to?"

Jessica was still reeling from the absurdity of it all but she could see that

Dr. Pham was not going to believe her if she continued to deny. She just wanted to get out of there and go home.

"No, I don't, I mean, I used to but I don't know..." There was no way she was going to waste more time at an OB/GYN when there was no earthly way she was pregnant unless it was another immaculate conception!

"I give you referral to OB/GYN, Miss Jessica. I print out referral and some 'scripts for you to get some prenatal vitamins and iron and you get to the baby doctor! Okay, you understand?"

Jessica nodded. "Would a pregnancy make me feel so sick that I have to be rushed to the hospital?"

Dr. Pham leaned over and stared in her face as if she was about to reveal some deep secret.

"Yes, it will if you're under nourished and low in iron and all of the things a baby needs to grow. Babies just suck up everything inside of you! You need more to live! You need extra cause baby is now taking it all! Greedy babies!

They greedy before they even born!" Dr. Pham roared with laughter.

I'm not pregnant." Jessica said to herself, seeing that it was useless to keep disputing the doctor. She would just get a second opinion. But first she needed to get out of there.

"Yep, you're pregnant!" declared Dr. Ogletree.

"What? How?" asked Jessica as she sat on the exam table two weeks later. Her breasts felt heavy and sore and having to be braless for the examination made them hang uncomfortably under the thin gown. Her nipples were extremely hard and the rough cotton sheet felt painful brushing against them.

"Um, *how?*" Dr. Ogletree looked at her, bemused. "Are you playing with me right now?"

His nurse stood a few feet away, scribbling into her chart. The conversation caught her attention and she piped in.

"Is this your first child, Miss Gordon? I just had my first child too; she's only three months and I just came back to work! I can give you lots of information to help you!" She said with a perky tone that made Jessica want to leap from the table and smash her in her face with the clipboard.

"No thank you, I don't need any information because I can't be pregnant, dammit! I just had sex two freaking weeks ago! What is wrong with you people and your stupid tests? If anything, I'm two freaking weeks pregnant and I don't even think that would show up yet!"

Dr. Ogletree cleared his throat uncomfortably and scratched the top of his white-haired head. He looked over at his nurse as if he wanted her to back him up.

"Miss Gordon, the tests show that you are about 16 weeks pregnant. Not two." He paused to gauge her reaction. "I know you told my nurse that your last menstrual cycle was approximately three weeks ago, but to be sure, we sent both your urine and blood specimens for lab work and it came back conclusive."

He took a step back and stuck out his hand for the nurse to pass him the brown medical file. She stuck it nervously into his hand and he opened it and flipped through the pages before he continued.

"I also examined you myself, I examined your cervix and I estimated you to be 16 to 18 weeks gestation based on the results of my observation of your cervix as well as the size of the apparent fetus you are carrying in your belly." Dr. Ogletree sounded a little annoyed at the fact that Jessica was questioning his knowledge and capabilities as a medical professional. He handed the file back to his nurse and turned to Jessica again.

"While it's clear to everyone with eyes that you are carrying a child in your belly - would you like us to conduct an ultrasound? You have not had one yet and you are allowed two during the course of the pregnancy for the safety of the child. You are due for one at this point but apparently your refusal to believe you are pregnant has kept you from having the first," Dr. He crossed his arms and waited for her response.

Jessica nodded weakly and apologized. This was a nightmare and she didn't know how to wake up. "I'm sorry, Dr. Ogletree. I really don't mean to be rude or question you. I'm just really not understanding this and not prepared. It makes no sense. But yes, I'd like an ultrasound as soon as possible."

"Would you please excuse us?" Dr. Ogletree signaled for the nurse to follow him out of the room, and Jessica could hear them standing outside of the exam room door speaking in hushed tones.

She rubbed her hands across her protruding belly. Yes, it was growing bigger and bigger each day, and yes, she was still experiencing morning sickness and weird cravings and sleeping nearly 10 hours every night. Her ankles were often swollen after a long day at work and she wanted to eat everything in sight, but she refused to believe she was carrying a baby inside. Perhaps it was a tumor. A fast growing deadly cancerous tumor that had wrapped itself around her liver and was feeding off of her like a succubus. Somehow, the idea of a cancerous tumor seemed like a better option than a child. But wouldn't cancer have shown up in all of the many lab tests she had been subjected to between this now THIRD doctor?

In the room alone, she lay back on the exam table and pulled apart the white gown. She felt along the circumference of her belly and stroked the smooth skin of the growth that was now the size of a small watermelon. She had managed to hide it well beneath her work clothing, committing to wearing mostly oversize smocks and tunics paired with blazers that provided camouflage. But it was becoming increasingly difficult to keep her slacks above her hips since she could no longer fasten or zip them, having instead to use a belt to hold keep them from falling down and tripping her.

She pressed her fingers into the mound, gently at first, and then because she didn't feel anything, she used even more pressure; she moved the position of her hands and pressed again, just past the point of pain, and she suddenly felt something shift inside. She gasped and cried out, jerking her hands up in the air away from her own body. She held as still as she could, not even breathing, and she felt it again. It moved. It *scurried*. From one side of her belly to the other.

She slowly returned her hands to her belly and cupped both sides, and after a few seconds, she felt the pressure of a poke from the inside, pushing against the surface of her skin as if it were trying to match her hands, to touch her, to join hands with her through her body. She recoiled in horror as she felt a tiny lump rise in her belly and move beneath her hand, searching and prodding, exploring.

She looked down and saw something poking up, like a thumb poking from the inside; she felt it dragging around on the interior of her body, almost as if it were drawing letters on a chalkboard, signaling her, trying to communicate with her. Panicked, she took her hand and slapped the lump hard, once, twice, until it disappeared beneath her skin, then began poking on the opposite side of her stomach. She reached over and used her fists to punch that lump down as hard as she could, gasping at the impact of being punched in the stomach, even if it were by her own fists.

She heard what sounded like a muffled screech of a cat and the *baby* inside punched back with the force of an angry punch by a small child - only it really hurt coming from the inside of where her organs resided!

She held her breath, afraid to move for fear of alerting the doctor and nurse and they would think she was a lunatic and have her put on a 72 hour hold.

Jessica swallowed hard as she realized that the doctors were right about one thing. There was something inside of her. It was alive. And she had made it angry.

She had taken a personal leave from work so that she could take care of her problem. She had been with the company for 10 years and was well-respected in her role as creative director, so she had both unused vacation and plenty of paid medical leave to afford to handle her business as necessary. However, paid medical leave required doctor's affirmation and consent, and where she was going would not qualify as a legitimate medical facility, not unless Sheila Boom Boom had saved all of the money from those teenage abortions and took harass to medical school.

It had become nothing less than impossible to hide her bulging belly without looking totally ridiculous; and she refused to resort to maternity clothing and have the entire company questioning when she was due and planning an office baby shower and setting up those dreadful baby pools. She knew it was time to call it quits when the lady that worked the pizza counter in the cafeteria gave her an extra slice for free, winked at her, and told her to feed that baby.

Jessica threw away her tray of pizza and ran to the restroom stall for a good cry. It wasn't as if she hadn't noticed the stares or heard the whispers around the building as she walked by. They all knew, especially the women, they knew but were waiting for her to tell them the "*good news.*" Well, those bitches could wait because there was not going to be any baby news coming from her way.

After the cafeteria incident, she marched up to HR and requested a private meeting with the manager, where she tearfully poured out a story about a deadly stomach cancer that ran in her family and how she had been in complete denial for so long, but had finally resigned herself to accept the inevitable chemo and radiation treatments to eradicate the cancer and destroy the growing tumor in her belly..

She knew her story would not go beyond the walls of HR or she would own that company, so she went home that day feeling like a weight had been lifted off of her shoulders as she looked over at the medical leave papers in the passenger's seat of her car.

Best case scenario, she'd fake a miscarriage and get her doctor to assign her to bed rest, after which she could return to work minus a baby that no one would be callous enough to ask about.

There was no doctor that would perform an abortion this late in her...pregnancy, as it were, since they insisted that she was now nearing all of seven months, even though it had only been about four weeks since Steve shot his unholy sperm inside of her canal. Whatever. They could keep twisting the truth anyway they pleased, it no longer mattered. She had made up her mind. For whatever reason she had been *blessed* with this creature growing inside of her, she was not going to keep it. Period.

It grew in ways unexplainable; it curled and stretched and taunted and teased her when she was sleeping; poking and scraping along her walls with something that felt like a sharp fingernail, dragging it along the membrane as if it wanted out. She felt it kick; she thought she heard it *scream* in the middle of the night when everything was quiet. She thought it heard it *laugh* when she immersed herself in a tub of water as hot as she could stand it, hoping to overheat the little fucker and make it die from a fever. She lay on top of it once, by accident, and felt it move into her spine and start kicking at her vertebra until the pain forced her to roll over to her side. She jumped up and down on a little cardio-trampoline she purchased at the sporting goods store, and when she jumped, she could feel it bouncing around inside and she hoped to shake it up so bad that it would break its little demonic neck. But when she stopped jumping, she felt it grab hold to the umbilical cord and snatch it hard against her belly button, causing her to cry out in pain.

She tried everything she could to make its little life miserable, and it punished her in every way it could imagine from inside. It became a battle of wills between the two, but she was still the biggest and the strongest and dammit - *she* would win.

She had a plan for it. A plan so good that she was almost afraid to think about it because she feared that *it* could read her thoughts. But her plan involved her old friend Sheila Boom Boom. The woman who helped her out when she was a young girl, pregnant and frightened, who came to her with the money she'd borrowed from her friends and stolen from the wallet of that married bastard who impregnated her. Now, she was a woman with a problem and a lot of money to fix it. She had no doubt that she could get Sheila Boom Boom to help her when no one else would.

Steve had stayed true to form and didn't disappoint. Jessica expected nothing from him and that's what she received, exactly nothing. He didn't even call back to see if she had made it safely to the hospital or if she was feeling better. He didn't even attempt to try to call to hook up another date. Whatever itch he had that compelled him to call a month ago, well, she scratched it for him and now he had returned to his life with his babe.

Jessica tried his number one final time, her mind racing as she tried to rehearse what she would say if and when he answered. She didn't even know why she felt the need to even hear his voice, it was not as if she was going to keep the thing; she wasn't hoping for him to have a change of heart and collapse in a fit of tears and beg for her forgiveness. No, it was just a morbid curiosity that she couldn't shake: if he really had changed and was trying to reconcile with her, had she blown it by kicking him out so crudely after they'd had sex? Did it matter anyway? She wasn't interested in giving him another chance to trample and piss all over her life the way he had done in the past. Whether or not she carried his seed would not change who he had been - or what he was. She hated him with the passion of a thousand suns and if whatever this was growing inside of her had anything to do with him, she hated it too.

But she had to hear his voice anyway.

When he answered, everything she rehearsed slipped out of her mind and she found herself choking back tears.

"Steve?"

"Yeah? What?" He responded coldly.

"How are you?"

"Um, fine. Why?"

Jessica paused. "Well, I hadn't heard from you so I was just checking."

"You didn't want to hear from me, remember?"

"I know, I know, I'm sorry, I wasn't nice to you and you...you didn't deserve that." It pained her to utter those words of contrition, especially when he did indeed deserve it.

Steve cleared his throat. "So did you want something, Jess? Is there a reason you're calling me now?"

She hesitated, and then continued. "I just wanted to ask you - how could things have been different between us? I mean, it really doesn't change anything now, but I just wonder sometimes, what happened? We were good together, a long time ago."

"What happened? You don't know how to let a man be a man, that's what happened," replied Steve dryly. "You're never gonna be happy with a man until you stop trying to BE the man."

Jessica had to fight back laughter and resist the urge to launch into a tirade about what a pathetic excuse for a man he really was, but she knew it would be a waste of her breath. Besides, little Junior had started twisting and turning at the sound of his voice coming through the phone; warning her that one false move would jeopardize her organs.

"I won't bother you again, Steve, take care," she said, and winced as he disconnected their call before she could press the button herself.

"Girl, look at you!" Angel exclaimed as she attempted to wrap her arms around Jessica's huge belly. It was now the size of a full-term pregnancy and Jessica had no choice but to allow it to lead her as she arched her back and followed. The pain in her lower back was often so bad that she gave in and bought a medical brace that would lift her large belly and take the pressure off of her spine. She grimaced and eased her wide hips and butt into the chair and slid back to make room for the belly.

"Are you sure you're not having twins? Or triplets?" Angel was wide-eyed with excitement. "You are HUGE! There's no way there's just one baby in there! What does your doctor say?"

"It's just one, trust me," replied Jessica. She couldn't admit to Angel that she was no longer seeing a doctor. She didn't want to be lectured or warned about how she needed prenatal care and how the baby needed this or that. She gave up on doctors when she couldn't find one that would dig deeper into this Immaculate Conception of which she was a victim. They all looked at her as if she were crazy and shook their head pitifully, thinking that she was just in denial about some failed relationship and was attempting to wish it away. She even began to doubt herself - did she get drunk one night while out with her friends and end up drugged and raped? Other than the dinner date with Steve, she couldn't even recall having more than one drink in the last few months because she had been under such enormous pressure to complete a project at work, so on the occasion that she went out, she only allowed herself a tiny bit of escapism and then it was off to bed so she could rise early and get back to work. She was so perplexed by it all that she even wondered if perhaps one of the maintenance men at her apartment complex had used his key to enter at night, drug her and have his way with her, thus impregnating her. But surely she would have felt something when she woke the next morning.

She checked her body for unexplained needle marks or bruising, but other than the numerous pokes from the various doctors she had seen, she found nothing. Although her body was badly bruised from the many attempts she made at throwing herself down the stairs to end this farce of a pregnancy. She ran into the walls at full speed and bounced off her belly; she opened the kitchen drawers with all of her force and slammed it into her belly; nothing bothered that evil fetus inside of her. It would curl up in a knot near her side and wait patiently for her to finish her games, and then it would kick and claw and yell for hours, running back and forth inside of her like a mouse, causing her to retch violently and beg tearfully for forgiveness before it would finally give her peace.

"How far along are you?"

Jessica rubbed her stomach and felt it kick as if to warn her not to start that shit again about not being pregnant. It hated when she tried to pretend like it didn't exist. *Dammit, I'm here and I'm coming, so deal!* It seemed to taunt her.

"Um, I think about 7 or 8 months - how far do you think I look?"

"Don't you know? Don't you have a due date yet? We need to plan the baby shower but you haven't been calling me. Is everything okay?"

It moved again, waking up, stretching and listening.

"Yes, its fine, I'm fine, just tired most of the time. I'm sorry; I don't mean to ignore you. You know you're my girl, I miss you," Jessica's voice cracked and it kicked her to remind her to stay in character. She felt sharp prick in what felt like her kidney, that was a warning shot. Clean up the tears, Jessica, don't make me show my ass.

"Aw, hun, you know I'm here for you! Don't try to do this alone, I got you, sis," Angel reached across the table and grabbed Jessica's hand.

She fought back tears and smiled. "This is my first pregnancy you know, us pregnant women get all emotional and shit, don't mind me. I'm just really big and tired and ready to get this over with so I can have my body back."

Another warning kick.

The waiter arrived to take their orders and Jessica suddenly had an idea.

"Can I have a blue margarita?" She asked the young waiter and he looked at her as if she had two heads.

"Well, yeah, I can get you a virgin blue margarita," he said after a moment of surprise left his face.

"No, I don't want a virgin anything, I want a real margarita. Will you do that for me?" Jessica reached into her bag and pulled out a folded twenty-dollar bill, sliding it toward the young man underneath her fingers.

It stabbed her viciously in her spine and she jumped and changed position in her chair, ignoring the pain.

"Jess!" Angel gasped and grabbed for the money. "What is wrong with you?"

"Just one, please, I just need it, one won't hurt!" Jessica whined, nearing tears.

"I'm sorry, ma'am but I could lose my job, I don't think I can do that." He rolled his eyes and then looked at Angel. "Are you ready to place your order or would you like a little more time?"

"A little more time, please, "spoke Angel, then sat back in her chair and glared at Jessica.

"I'm sorry," Jessica spoke after the waiter left the table, dropping her eyes. "I just feel like I need something to take off the edge. I'm so scared right now. I'm getting closer to the due date and I'm honestly petrified of the pain and everything that's going to change in my life. I just wanted a little taste of something strong to help me relax."

She had tried to purchase liquor at other times but was always met with disapproving eyes from the counter clerk. She thought about driving out to the liquor store in her old neighborhood where they question nothing as long as the money is real. They would sell you an Uzi and a young Mexican virgin over the counter as long as you had the money in hand. She could certainly go there to get all of the liquor she needed to drink herself into a dangerous state of intoxication that would expel this hell-baby from inside of her.

The only drawback is that she herself did not want to die, and she would have to go to the hospital in order to save her own life, and that would lead to questions and possibly an investigation and criminal charges. So that plan had too many holes to be successful. Besides, that little monster would probably enjoy the alcohol and suck it all up and start dancing; it might become even meaner than it already was and she didn't want that.

"It's almost over, don't worry, just hang in there."

"Oh, I know, it is almost over," agreed Jessica.

The waiter returned and Jessica placed an order of chicken fingers, fries, onion rings and garlic bread. She wanted to starve the little bastard but she was too hungry to think about that plan.

Angel cleared her throat. "So, um, are you going to ever tell me who the father is? Or is that something you plan to just keep secret forever? Are you embarrassed by it? I mean, you don't have to be, girl, I get it! We've all had those moments of regret, you get lonely and hook up with someone and can't believe you did it later!"

"It wasn't like that at all."

"Were you already seeing Steve when you told me about your date? Was that really not your first time seeing him in months but you just didn't know how to break it to me? Because we're girls, you know I would never judge you like that, you could have told me if you were sneaking around with him. I wouldn't have liked it but I would have understood."

"Would you? Would you really?" Jessica was becoming agitated. "You say that now, but would you really?"

"Yes, of course, if that's what you really wanted. I would have tried to talk you out of it because I'm your friend and friends don't let friends make stupid decisions."

"So you agree it was a stupid decision?"

"What do you think, Jess? Do you not have any regrets?"

Another tug at her insides. *Why doesn't it just go to sleep?*

"I no longer have regrets. Too late for that now," replied Jessica, rolling her eyes. "What's done is done."

Perhaps it was going to be easier to just let Angel believe that Steve was the father rather than being secretive about it.

"I wanted to tell you back when I first found out -"

"-and when exactly was that? Because it's been like six weeks since you told me you were going on your date with him so he could see what he's been missing, and somehow you managed to hide all of this - " Angel waved her hands in the air over Jessica's stomach. "I don't know how but one day you're skinny as a rail and now you're just full of baby and ass. That's a fast growing little heffa you got there! Probably going to be a football player like its daddy, huh?"

"Yeah, whatever," Jessica said. "But if I was in my right mind, back when I found out, I mean *early* in, I would have been paying our old friend Sheila Boom Boom a visit."

"Who?"

"You remember, Sheila from the city? Sheila Boom Boom? She used to hook everybody up, with that thick Jamaican accent? She said we all come to her when we do too much boom boom?"

Angel looked around as if she was afraid that someone might hear her. "Oh my God, Jess, I can't believe you would even say her name in public like that. I thought you never wanted to talk about that again?"

"Well, it's been years now, what's the big deal anymore."

"The big deal? She almost killed you! That nasty little place and those dirty instruments of torture! Have you forgotten?"

Jessica rolled her eyes. "Hey, she served a purpose. Just because mine didn't work out well doesn't mean she didn't do a lot of good for a lot of young, scared girls. A lot of our friends who are lawyers and doctors and executives today might not be that if it weren't for Sheila Boom Boom helping them out. They'd probably be poor and with a house full of kids, wishing they'd done things differently."

"Okay, I'll give you that much, but why would you consider going to her when you've got a good job and insurance and abortion is legal - you're an adult, it's not like you need your parent's approval."

"Because Sheila knows how to keep her mouth shut and there's no records. If I go anywhere else - especially if I use my insurance, there's a record waiting for someone to read it and use it against me."

Angel laughed. "Use it against you how? You planning to run for president? Your medical records are private."

"Yeah, private until somebody hacks into the system and then blackmails me."

"You are a mess. Okay, I get that, but Sheila was dangerous, she had to be stopped. She could have killed people, she almost killed you!"

"Was she stopped? I mean, did she get arrested or something?"

"No, I think she just stopped herself, too much heat was coming down on her, rumors and stuff; it was only a matter of time before someone went to the police. Last I heard, she was still living in the same place. Someone said on Facebook that they saw her in the store and recognized her and she went rushing away like she was scared."

Jessica attempted to conceal her smile at that bit of news. It was exactly what she needed to hear but she couldn't risk *it* knowing that she was setting a plan into motion. Their food arrived and for the first time, she enjoyed her meal and kept the conversation light-hearted and casual, cleverly avoiding discussion about baby showers or baby room decorations or anything related to *it's* future. She made sure to keep her mind clear of unpleasant thoughts surrounding impending motherhood.

As she got closer to an empty plate, she could feel the weight in her stomach drop and settle, as if it were eating the food along with her. She had gotten rather used to the feeling of it moving around inside of her like a squirrel; she could even anticipate its actions in relation to her own. It would flutter and roll in the morning when she awoke, perch and tap on her walls when she was in a discussion with anyone, and stretch and kick when she was doing housecleaning, as if it felt she was moving around too much.

This time, it dropped into her cervix with a slight thud and after a few moments of stillness, she began to feel intense pressure in her bowels, and she quickly muttered her apologies to Angel and rushed toward the front entrance of the restaurant, searching frantically for the restroom. The hostess stationed at the front podium saw her distress and pointed her in the right direction.

Jessica pushed through the restroom door and ran into the first stall as she hurried to loosen her clothing. The pressure in her lower area increased and she landed on the toilet seat with both relief and fear.

Was it going to push itself out? She wondered as panic began to build in her chest. That would be one way out of this: let it come out in the toilet and flush the bastard away! Her stomach bubbled and she leaned forward to rest her elbows on her knees, feeling the urge to push.

She was grateful that there was no one else in the restroom at the time because a searing pain forged through the lower half of her body as she bore down and tried to expel whatever it was from her womb.

A gush of liquid escaped her body and splashed in the toilet bowl, and dizziness caused Jessica to grip the mobility bars on each side of the stall. She continued to press down until the urge to push had gone away. She sat still with her eyes closed, breathing deeply, feeling excited at the possibility of looking into the toilet and finding the end to her nightmare.

When she separated her legs and looked down, she gasped in horror. The water was blood red and contained what looked like hundreds of small lumps of meat, swaying gently on the surface of the stool.

Jessica collapsed on her knees and cried silently, not wanting to attract the attention of the restaurant staff or other patrons. She used the tissue to wipe herself and stood to fix her clothing when she noticed the slight movement in the toilet caught her eye. The small pink pieces were curling and stretching, almost *swimming* in the bloody water. Jessica leaned forward to examine the contents of the toilet more closely and then gasped in horror when she realized that the pieces of meat were plump maggots, twisting and turning in the stool.

She flushed the toilet and watched as they swirled around the bowl and down the drain; then flushed again to rinse away the stragglers.

When she opened the stall to clean her hands at the sink, she looked at herself in the mirror and nodded her head as if to answer her own questions.

There was only one way out now.

It could have gone a little smoother, but nevertheless, she achieved her goal. She lay on her bed rubbing her stomach, now nearly flat with a softly sloping rise beneath her navel and the extra fat from carrying the baby fell to her side. She smiled to herself as she recalled the day's events that scored her victory.

Three hours earlier, she had returned to the building where she last visited Sheila Boom Boom and took the elevator to the 12th floor. Memories washed over her as she waddled down the long hallway until she reached apartment 13, Sheila's old unit. She would never forget that apartment, the way it looked: grays and browns, everything gray and brown from either dust, darkness, or dinginess; the way it smelled; greasy, like someone regularly deep fried some undetermined animal, and medicinal, as if they poured alcohol on top of the meat after it was done frying.

Jessica stood on the other side of that door as she did 10 years ago, weighing the pros and cons of what she was about to do, rather, <u>attempt</u> to do. She almost turned around and rushed back down the hall to the elevator to disappear before the damage was done. <u>It</u> was twisting and turning and forced her to stop every few feet and hold on to the wall to calm herself. It knew what she was trying to do and it was fighting for its very survival.

When Sheila Boom Boom opened the door and saw Jessica's huge belly, her face at first showed confusion and she slowly brought her eyes up to Jessica's, seeking answers.

"Can I come in? I need to sit right now," Jessica spoke and her belly visibly shook and rumbled beneath the sheer maternity shirt. She grabbed it with both hands and stumbled back against the wall in the hallway.

The old woman stepped into the hall and reached out to offer her support, guiding her into the messy living room by the elbow. She could see Jessica's stomach lurching and shifting beneath the fabric and she was fascinated. As she helped Jessica ease into an upholstered chair, Jessica yelled in pain and she panicked, worried that she had left a syringe or a sharp tool on the cushion, but Jessica immediately settled back in the seat and started to stroke her rumbling stomach as it pitched and roared underneath her fingers.

"A wha dis, a labor yuh inna?" asked Sheila Boom Boom.

Jessica shook her head as tears squeezed from the corners of her eyes.

"You have to take this baby out of me," she whispered through clenched teeth. "It's trying to kill me. It's evil and I need it gone!"

Sheila reached out to touch the moving mass and snatched her hands back, recoiling in horror as a lump formed underneath the shirt and seemed to punch toward her.

"Wha yuh mean evil? What is that happening there?" She waved her hand across Jessica's belly and it continued to lurch and roll as if it were trying to follow the movement of her hand.

"I need it out now, dammit!" Jessica screamed. "It's not a fucking baby, its a monster - don't you see it? Do you see what it's doing? What baby acts like this? Look!"

She took her hands and gripped the edges of her shirt and angrily ripped it open, allowing the buttons to fly across the room as the fabric tore beneath her grip. She threw her head back and jammed her fist in her mouth to muffle her screams of anguish as the baby fought violently inside of her belly.

Sheila gasped in horror but couldn't take her eyes away; she wanted to run out of the apartment but her legs wouldn't move. Her eyes were fixed on Jessica's belly as it fought to contain the angry kicking baby inside. It reminded her of the time she watched her older brother place her beloved cat in a burlap bag and then tie the end to secure it. The cat fought and clawed and screamed for what seemed like hours, as her brother used his strong arms to keep her from getting close to it. She fell to the ground and cried in anguish until a neighbor overheard the commotion and came to rescue both her and the cat.

Jessica's belly moved in the same manner as that burlap bag holding a vicious animal trying to claw its way out. Sheila thought she could hear noises coming from inside of Jessica's belly, angry snarling noises that surely couldn't be from anything human.

Jessica tossed her head back and forth in pain, and the tidal wave of nausea caused drool to spill from the corners of her mouth. She took a deep breath and pitched forward in the chair and held still, staring at the floor and letting the saliva drip from her mouth to the floor. Sheila moved forward to place her hand on Jessica's shoulder but she turned her head and hissed at her, "Don't! Don't...touch...me! Wait!"

Sheila took a step back and just watched as Jessica held her position, compressing her stomach between her chest and knees. It became clear that she was squeezing the baby, limiting the amount of space it had to move around inside, forcing it to be still. After a few moments, she straightened her back and sat upright in the chair, looking at Sheila with pleading tearful eyes.

"You have to help me, Sheila, I don't know where else to turn! You used to help a lot of young girls years ago, I know because I was one of them," Jessica said.

Sheila shook her head and backed away. "No, no, I don't do that anymore! I stopped that a long time ago. I can't, they're watching me now, I can't do it. You need to go to a hospital!"

Jessica laughed ruefully. "A hospital? What do you think they will do? They can't help me! Why in the hell do you think I'm here?"

"What you want? You want to go into labor? You want me to make you go into labor? I can show you how - I can't do it for you!" Sheila's eyes were wide and fearful as she watched Jessica's belly come to life. She saw it start to shake and jump as if the baby was again waking up.

Jessica felt it too. She rolled sideways in the chair and began to vomit onto the carpeted floor; pools of red blood mixed with multi-colored bits of food and liquid shot out from her mouth and hit the floor, splattering the sides of the chair and the legs of the table sitting within reach.

Sheila hurried to the kitchen to grab some paper towels, muttering to herself, "Crazy old girl! I don't know why you come here! I can't help you. I don't deliver babies!"

When she returned, Jessica was on her hands and knees with her head hanging over the steaming puddle of vomit. Her body convulsed as it tried to produce more but her stomach was empty. She tried to speak in between the retching.

"Cut the shit, Sheila! We both know what you do! This isn't much different! It's gonna kill me if you don't help!" she cried.

Sheila thrust the roll of paper towel in her face with one hand and offered her other hand to rise from the floor.

"I will show you how to go into labor, but the rest you have to do it yourself. I'm not going to jail for you," said Sheila.

Once Jessica returned to the chair, she pulled Sheila down to her face. "That's fine, but whatever I do once it's out, stays here, between us. I know what you used to do and I know enough people who aren't afraid to come forward about it now."

She screamed in pain as the baby kicked out with such force that Sheila jumped at the same time.

"Okay, okay!" Sheila rushed back to the kitchen and slammed a small pot on the stove. She turned the burner on Low and then stooped to reach deep into her cabinet and pull forth an aluminum breadbox that had seen better days. She went down to her knees, groaning at the stiffness in her bones as they settled on the hard linoleum floor. Setting the box on the floor in front of her, she bent and began removing bottles of liquid and bags of dried herbs, reaching up to place the selected items on the counter next to the warming pot.

When she had her ingredients assembled, she began to pour them into the pot; raspberry herb tea, castor oil, mineral oil, all went into the pot and rose to a simmer while Jessica moaned and cried softly from the other room.

When Sheila returned, Jessica was nearly delirious from the pain that the baby was inflicting on her from inside as it fought to stay alive. It knew that its time was near and it was going to live or kill her trying. Jessica wanted to just close her eyes and give up, but the fighter inside of her wouldn't allow her to surrender.

Sheila approached her with a wide mug of a steamy foul smelling liquid that resembled raw sewage. She thrust the mug in front of Jessica's face and she gagged at the disgusting odor.

"Drink this! Drink it quick so you can get out of my house with whatever it is you have in your belly!" Sheila hissed at her.

Jessica took the mug with both hands and held her breath as she tried to take a sip, but as soon as the liquid touched her tongue, it assaulted every one of her senses and her body rejected it. The baby began screaming and shaking as her taste buds signaled her brain that the ingredients forthcoming were not meant for human consumption - but they were coming in anyway.

Sheila ran out of the room again and returned holding an armful of blankets which she used to pad the sofa.

"Come here and sit while you drink so you can lie down when it starts!" Sheila commanded.

"It's that fast?" Jessica asked between gasps of pain.

"As soon as it get inside you - drink!"

"I can't, I thought I could but I can't, its horrid!"

"So is that thing inside of you - drink!" Sheila yelled.

Jessica sucked in as much air as she could, pinched her nose with her left hand and turned up the bowl, gulping it down as quickly as she could. After a few swallows, it tried to come rushing back up out of her stomach, but she could see the finish line and she was not going to stop. She swallowed it back down and continued forcing the rest of the contents of the mug to go down her throat.

She suddenly tossed the empty mug onto the floor and gripped the arms of the chair as the first wave hit her. Out of the corner of her eye, she saw Sheila reach for her and she allowed herself to be lead to the padded sofa. Sheila stretched her out and began removing her clothing and she went limp, knowing that it would be over soon if she just held on.

Muffled screams rose from her belly; it screeched and wailed as if it were on fire, and kicked against her spine in an effort to hurt her as much as she was hurting it.

Sheila managed to get her completely naked and then threw a warm blanket across her body. Jessica felt her lower body being wrenched up in the air and plastic garbage bags pushed underneath her behind. Sheila sat a bucket of water and a pile of rags on the floor next to the sofa, then dropped to her knees next to Jessica, pulling the blanket down beneath her breasts.

Jessica watched wearily from behind clouded eyes as Sheila reached up and pulled dentures from her mouth with a wet sucking sound, placing them on the table near Jessica's head. Her mind began racing with questions when she suddenly felt Sheila's ragged wet lips at her nipple, pulling and sucking, while another bony hand skipped across her chest to pinch at her other nipple.

Confused and scared, she opened her mouth to protest but the woman kept suckling at her as if she was nursing, but she would turn her head every few minutes and spit into the bucket on the floor. She continued sucking on Jessica's nipple and stimulating the other until Jessica felt a wave of pain race through her lower stomach that caused her to scream at the top of her lungs.

"Shut up!" Sheila admonished her. "You wanted this now shut up!"

Jessica struggled to keep her eyes open but the pain was becoming too much. The room went black and she went happily toward the darkness.

Jessica stumbled from the tiny apartment with a blood-soaked maxi-pad in her underwear. She felt dizzy and weak, even after resting in Sheila's bed, and the enormous loss of blood made her feel lethargic, but she just wanted to get to her bed where she could sleep for the rest of the night. The pad needed changing already and she feared that she might not make it home without it overflowing and running down her legs, but it was a chance she would have to take. She shouldn't be driving, but she was going to inch her way home, slowly, and hope that she made it without hurting herself or others.

She could still hear the screams. She imagined it would be a while before she could clear her head of that horrible sound. It still screamed as she held it under the water. It was easier than she thought it would be, to hold it, to drown it. She thought she would freeze up and chicken out, but when she saw its tiny shriveled body, jet black and rubbery like the fetus of a Doberman - that made it easier to do what she had to do. It wasn't a child, as she believed all along. It was a...thing. An evil thing. Something inhuman and vile. It had tiny red eyes and a slithery forked tongue that it stuck out and hissed at her as she lowered it into the mop bucket. It was strong but not as strong as her. She used both hands to hold it down and tighten her grip around its tiny throat at the same time, until bubbles formed on the surface of the water. Then she knew it was safe to let go.

Sheila sat on the floor and rocked back and forth, praying softly and crying. She refused to watch, she didn't want to see or know what was happening. She kept her eyes focused on the floor in front of her. She didn't even look up when Jessica said, "It's done."

"Finish it," Sheila said. "Get it out of here and you leave too!"

Jessica moved slowly; she felt soreness between her legs from expelling the...thing...but since it was smaller than they expected, Sheila assured her that she wouldn't need stitches. She had left an envelope on Sheila's table containing 20 one-hundred dollar bills, for her help and her silence - much more than she had paid her when she was a frightened teenager, but then, the cost of her sins ran much higher these days.

She made it home in time to change the pad before it spilled over and made a mess of the interior of her car. After taking another of the powerful painkillers supplied by Sheila, she felt a sense of relief wash over her as she stood in the quiet of her bedroom and realized that she was alone. She collapsed on the bed, face first, flat on her stomach, and sank deep into the first truly peaceful sleep she'd had in two months.

Six Months Later

Jessica woke to the sound of her alarm and sprung out of bed in a panic. She normally woke right on time to her internal clock, but lately she had been sleeping much more deeply, and the black curtains on her window stayed drawn tightly so she didn't sense the dawn when it arrived.

Candles flickered around the bedroom, in various stages of burning out after several hours of filling the room with fragrance. Jessica stopped to relight some of the candles as she passed on her way to the shower.

A handful of flies buzzed around the bathroom mirror and she shooed them away with a frown before she turned on the hot water and tested it with her hand.

A candle sat on the back of the toilet and she picked up the lighter next to it and light the wick.

A hot steamy shower was just what she needed to wake completely and prepare for the day at work. She stepped into the shower, humming a jingle from a commercial she'd heard on the radio. The spray from the showerhead felt revitalizing as it beat down on her face like a million tiny needles. She worked up a rich lather with the soap and scrubbed her arms and legs, sweeping the soapy loofah across the swollen mound of her lower belly.

After the shower, she stood in front of the full-length mirror in her bedroom and applied perfumed lotion to every inch of her body, then spritzed with a light fragrance. Sometimes, she could still smell the faint odor of something rotten in her skin, even after several layers of lotion, powder and perfume. It bothered her so much that she carried tiny bottles of oil in her bag and applied it throughout the day, especially if someone walked past and made a face as if they'd smelled something objectionable – or if she thought she made a face.

Down in the kitchen, air fresheners hanging from the ceiling tiles brushed her head as she drifted toward the counter to fix her lunch. She stopped at the sink and studied the glass jars lined up along the counter.

"Good morning, my pumpkins," she said cheerfully, tapping the jar closest to her. The fetus floated in the glass, suspended in a cloudy liquid; its tiny body was shriveled and only partially formed, with nubs where its arms and legs should be. A row of tiny sharp teeth was visible in the open hole in its face where a mouth should be. It wasn't alive, it never really lived, but it was clear from the expression on its unfinished face that it died in a fit of rage.

Jessica picked up another jar and shook it violently, her laughter rippling through the apartment.

"What's the matter? Don't be rude, you can't say good morning to Mommy?"

She gasped when she felt that familiar, eerie fluttering in her belly, as something scooted from the left side of her body to the right, then back again. Tiny fingers wiggled and poked at the top of her cervix and she squirmed, pressing her legs together.

"Stop it!" She yelled and gripped the edge of the counter. She opened the cabinet and withdrew a clean jar and slammed it on the counter, then rustled through the drawer and located the matching lid, setting it on the counter next to the jar.

"I'll take care of you later – don't worry, I've got your home ready for you!" Jessica laughed again.

She quickly threw together a lunch and stuffed it into a brown paper bag, then wrote herself a note on the fridge whiteboard to pick up more Mason jars at the hardware store.

Acknowledgments

This book was truly a labor of love, because it allowed me to do something I've been wanting to do for a long time – really let it all hang out and indulge myself in my favorite genre. There are no rules in horror – it's whatever you can dream; it doesn't have to be logical or even possible – in fact, the more illogical and impossible, the better!

My son, Joseph – thank you for listening to my story ideas (or even pretending to listen) and helping me shape and develop them for public consumption. I don't know what I would do without your 'thumbs up' or 'thumbs down' signals while your eyes are glued to your iPhone. Oh, and yes, you can read *this* book.

About Kenya

As a child, Kenya realized that her entertainment choices leaned more toward ghosts and goblins than princesses and fairy godmothers. She began writing short-form horror in her teens but didn't release her first book until many years later, thanks to the beauty of self-publishing. Although she may occasionally drop a work of romance, her real passion is weaving stories about monsters – both the kind that come from the pits of hell or may just be your neighbor.

When not staring at a blank page trying to conjure up the words, you might find Kenya shooting at the undead in her VR headset. Fun fact – Kenya collects Funko Pops of black horror movie icons.

Learn more about Kenya by visiting her social media listed on the **Find Me. Follow Me.** page.

Join My Mailing List

Only three quick steps to sign up for my mailing list and stay up to date on new releases, book events, sales and everything else! Visit the easy-to-remember site below, fill out two fields and you're in!

http://tinyurl.com/KMD-Mailing-List

More by Kenya

Horror/Thriller
Sick xoxo
The Mixtape
Prey for Me
Seed (coming soon)

Dark Fantasy
Madre (coming soon)
The Forever Souls

Anthologies
The Freestyle Cypher
Black Magic Women: Terrifying Tales by Scary Sisters
Forever Vacancy
Deadly Bargain

Nonfiction
160 Black Women in Horror

Romance
A Good Wife: The Whole Story

Get SICK with me!

Sick xoxo is the newest collection of horror stories from Kenya Moss-Dyme. She calls herself the 'Nightmare Vendor' and with this collection, you'll find out why! These stories are rooted in love, sex and death – the ultimate horror triad.

The honeymoon is over, let's get sick!

Get "Sick xoxo" in ebook or paperback at Amazon, or get a signed copy by visiting www.kenyamossdyme.com.

Reviews matter.

If you enjoyed this book, would you please leave me a review? Just a line or two would help, or even a star rating. If you purchased this book directly from me, please consider spreading the word with other readers.

If you didn't enjoy this book, I'd like to know what I can do better to win you over.

Thank you for reading!

Find Me. Follow Me.

Facebook: author.kenyamossdyme
Youtube: @KenyaMossDyme
TikTok: @kenyamossdyme
Instagram: kenyamossdyme
Email: kenya.mossdyme@gmail.com
Website: www.kenyawrites.com

#NSFW (Not Safe for Wimps)

Made in the USA
Columbia, SC
04 September 2024

41750127R00161